THE GIRL UNLEASHED

THE GIRL UNLEASHED

THE LAST VAMPIRE™ BOOK 5

JUDITH BERENS   MARTHA CARR   MICHAEL ANDERLE

DISRUPTIVE IMAGINATION®

LMBPN Publishing
PMB 196, 2540 South Maryland Pkwy
Las Vegas, NV 89109

First US edition, August 2019
eBook ISBN: 978-1-64202-415-9
Print ISBN: 978-1-64202-416-6

Thanks to the JIT Team

Jeff Goode
Paul Westman
Angel LaVey
Micky Cocker
Daniel Weigert
Dorothy Lloyd

If we've missed anyone, please let us know!

Editor
SkyHunter Editing Team

DEDICATIONS

From Martha

To everyone who still believes in magic
and all the possibilities that holds.
To all the readers who make this
entire ride so much fun.
And to my son, Louie and so many wonderful friends who
remind me all the time of what
really matters and how wonderful
life can be in any given moment.

From Michael

To Family, Friends and
Those Who Love
To Read.
May We All Enjoy Grace
To Live The Life We Are
Called.

CHAPTER ONE

Craig grunted as he yanked on the pull chain and the snowblower engine roared to life. He pulled his gloves on tighter and pushed down the lever to move the machine forward into the waist-high snow that had blown in front of the garage.

The drift was so high and thick that he could barely get the garage door to open. He shook his head in frustration while the spinning auger carved into the obstacle, chewed up the snow, and ejected it from the chute toward the back yard.

Unfortunately, the engine choked on the sheer mass of the snow it had to contend with. It wheezed and died—the third time it had done so since he came out to clear the driveway.

Almost out of breath, he hauled the equipment back into the garage and stepped around it until he was behind the drift. He admired the small rectangular dent the snow-blower managed to make before it died again.

The wind howled and pelted him in the cheeks with stinging wet snow. *I can't believe how hard this is coming down! Geez. I can barely see the house from here.*

He spun to take another look at the snowblower and sighed heavily. *The old girl can't handle this much snow. It's no use.* With a glum shake of his head, he stepped inside and shoved it back into the shed at the back of the garage.

His feet sank into the knee-deep snow at the low point of the drift when he stalked out of the garage and headed to the side door of the house. He squinted his eyes, which began to water. *Man, it's stupid cold. It feels like January out here.*

When he reached the back step, he turned to look at his footprints, some of which had already been partially filled in. *This is one heck of a blizzard.*

Vickie and Alexis greeted him at the door as he walked in and stomped the snow off his boots on the rug.

"That's it?" Vickie folded her arms. "I thought you were going to clear the snow."

Craig shook his head and laughed. "Yeah, that's not happening. My little snowblower is tough but even she can't handle how much is out there. We're getting dumped on right now." He peeled his snowsuit off and hung it on the hook and stepped into the kitchen while he rubbed his hands together and blew warm air across his skin. "It is seriously nasty out there. I haven't seen anything like it in years."

The vampire stepped over to the patio door and watched the snow blowing around and drifting all over the yard and the driveway. "Why did you go out now anyway? It's coming down so hard, you can't even see your footprints out there anymore. The driveway would be covered again by the time you were done."

He pulled a mug out from the cabinet and placed it on the counter. "My snowblower can't handle too much at once. During a blizzard like this, I usually go out in shifts. I clear a layer, let it build up, clear another layer, and so on. I guess I waited too long to go out there for the first round."

"Are we screwed, then?" Alexis asked and raised her eyebrows. "Stuck in here until it all melts?"

He laughed while he tore open a hot chocolate packet. "I don't know about that. But there's definitely consider-able work ahead of us. I'm not sure how we'll clear it all out. Honestly, it might take half a day and some shovels."

"On the bright side, we won't go to school today!" She pumped her fist.

Craig shook his head. "Thankfully, school is cancelled. I couldn't take you right now if you offered me a million dollars. No chance. I wouldn't be able to even get the back wheels of the SUV out of the garage."

Vickie tilted her head while she watched the snow swirl in the air. "I thought it was spring. Why do we have so much snow? It's April. Isn't April a time for warmer weather?"

"Not in Wisconsin." Alexis scoffed.

He filled his mug with water and slid it into the microwave. "In Wisconsin, you're never really safe from snow. Maybe when you reach June, you're safe for a few months."

"This is the latest I've seen this much snow, though." Alexis stood beside the other girl.

"The year after your mom and I were married, there

was a blizzard like this in May. Clearing it is the worst part. You can't do it like you would any other snowfall. There's so doggone much of it that you're kinda stuck."

His daughter pulled her phone out and opened her weather app. "But it looks like it'll warm up again in the next few days. Next week, it's supposed to be fifty degrees out. Maybe we should wait—"

"Nice try." After the microwave beeped, Craig withdrew his mug and lifted it to his lips to blow on it a little. "If we wait, we make all kinds of problems for ourselves. The snow starts to melt, and all that new water will sink to the bottom of the pile and be absorbed by it. It'll be ten times heavier and more impossible to lift."

"Can we simply wait until it melts completely?" Vickie turned to look at him. "If it's getting warmer, we don't really need to clear the driveway."

He took a sip of his hot chocolate. "Nope, that's not how it works either. Melting could take even longer. Sorry, girls, we can't avoid it. There'll be hard work needed to get us out of this. The school won't let you stay home for a week because of one day of snow."

Alexis grumbled a protest. "I hate shoveling. It seems like such a waste if you have a snowblower."

"I agree, but unless you're willing to buy me a nicer one that can handle this kind of weather, we'll be stuck here shoveling when we have this kind of a load dropped on us."

She shrugged. "I have a job now. How much is one of those fancy-pants snowblowers?"

Her father laughed as he joined them at the window and put his arm around her shoulder. "Something that can handle more than a foot of snow at a time without choking? I bet somewhere in the six-hundred-dollar range."

"Whoa!"

"Now you know why I use that little two-hundred-dollar one instead." He shook his head. "It sure is pretty. But it really stinks that I can't get this snow off the driveway now. It would make the work later much more manageable."

Vickie turned, walked to the side door, and retrieved her boots.

"What are you doing?" Alexis asked.

"I have an idea." She tied her boots and pulled her coat on. "Where is the shovel in there?"

Craig gave her a blank, confused stare. "It's just inside the garage door. Why?"

She smiled as she pulled her hat over her ears. "I'll be back in a minute." She stepped outside and slammed the back door shut behind her.

Father and daughter exchanged concerned glances.

"What do you think she's doing?"

"I have no clue." He sipped his hot chocolate. "But I hope she's careful out there. I don't know if vampires can freeze to death or not."

Outside, Vickie strode through the deep snow as she huddled forward to stay warm. When she reached the side door of the garage, she stepped in and closed it behind her, enveloping herself in darkness. *Whew. That really is coming down hard.* She pushed the button next to the door to open the big garage door again, and the brilliant white glare made her squint.

Vickie saw the shovel resting beside the door and picked it up. She dragged it to the middle of the opening just beyond the snow.

Okay, Vickie, let's see... If you try to do too much, you'll break the shovel on your first pass. It's not as strong as you. Test it first.

After she had taken a few digs into the drift and checked how much strain was put on the shovel, she stepped back and nodded. *It should be about three passes. You can work with that.*

While Craig and Alexis stared on with growing confusion, she waved at them and moved to the far end of the garage near the fence that lined the driveway. *I'll have to move from left to right, one row at a time. Push it toward the yard. Now, let's see if this will actually work.*

The vampire clutched the handle of the shovel, raised her chin, and closed her eyes to concentrate. As she breathed deeply and exhaled a fog of vapor into the frozen April air, she could feel the blood in her body begin to rush through her veins.

Her stomach tightened ever so slightly. *It's working. Only a little more.*

After a few more deep breaths, the hair on the back of her neck stood erect. She was ready.

In a flash, she shoveled the top layer of the snow off the driveway. A rapid flurry commenced, one scoop after another, until they all landed in a pile in the back yard.

She moved down the length of the driveway while father and daughter watched with their jaws hanging open. The rapid pace of her movements sounded like a loud hummingbird flapping her wings.

Within a few seconds, she had removed the top layer across the entire driveway. When she reached the end, she double-checked her senses to make sure no one was watching.

Nobody is outside within at least a few blocks. You're good.

She resumed her task and attacked the second layer along the length of the driveway, then turned and cleared all that remained to reveal the pavement beneath.

The entire driveway was cleared in under thirty seconds. She ran back to the garage to stand there and view the results of her work. *I cleared it before the snow had a chance to cover it again.* She nodded in approval, then looked at the bottom of the shovel.

It's melted a little right at the edge, which I suppose is to be expected with that kind of speed. But it's not too bad. The snow must have kept it from melting too much. Vickie returned the shovel to its place near the door, pressed the button to close it, and walked back to the house.

This time, she was met by Craig. "Holy cow! I almost dropped my mug watching that. Since when did you have that kind of control over your powers?"

Vickie shook her head as she kicked her boots off. "I took a chance. I haven't really tried to force it much, but it looks like I can do it. And now, I'm famished." She hung her coat and immediately went to the cupboard where they kept the snacks.

"Hey, eat what you want. You earned it, girl!" He patted her on the shoulder.

"This could really come in handy, Vickie." Alexis smiled. "If you have more control over your powers, we can put it to good use."

She shrugged as she stuffed a few potato chips in her mouth and walked to the fridge to get a drink.

CHAPTER TWO

Jim Trembo and Pete Stabone sat in a booth near the back of the Denny's diner across the street from the hotel they were staying in.

As they waited for their coffee and pancakes to arrive, Jim glanced out the window at the cars that inched their way slowly through the gridlock on the snow-covered freeway bridge. He laughed. "Days like these make me happy I don't have much of a commute." He flashed a white smile set perfectly in his chiseled jaw.

The other man's shoulders slumped while he tapped his foot. "Oh, yeah. I'm not a fan of walking around in this stuff, but it sure beats having to deal with all that traffic."

A waitress walked up and poured their coffees. Jim pulled his cup toward him and blew on it while his companion retrieved a few packets of sugar and a small cup of cream from the end of the table.

Pete whipped the packet briskly to settle the sugar to one side of the envelope. "I guess we're basically grounded today. There's no chance we'll make it out to the field in this weather."

Jim sighed. "Yeah. I'm bummed about it. Plus, we'll have to clear the area again from under all this snow. That will probably set us back a day or two."

He poured the sugar into his coffee. "Eh, what's another day or two? We've waited years for a result like this."

"You're not kidding." Jim took a sip of the bitter black coffee and puckered his lips. "There honestly is nothing like cheap diner coffee. Anyway, yeah, I know. I'm simply anxious to move this forward. We're finally hot on the trail of something big. There could be a whole race of...beings, I guess...out there in this part of the country that nobody knows about."

"It seems weird that they would be here, though. Wisconsin?" Pete poured the creamer into his coffee and stirred it with a spoon. "I know Milwaukee's not a big city compared to somewhere like New York, but if they're hiding out, why would they be here? I would think they would keep quiet somewhere in the middle of nowhere, like Canada."

"It depends on what they want, I suppose." The other man shrugged. "If their goals are to infiltrate society, it makes sense that they would choose a smaller city—a place they can get into rather quickly. Or maybe they simply need resources so they're hanging out here because they still have room to lay low without too many people asking questions." He sniffed as he looked around the diner. "And hey, Milwaukee might be a decent-sized city, but what else is there in Wisconsin? There are acres of wooded land in this state that no one really sees. Milwaukee could merely be their connection to civilization. There could be an underground population north of here. All possibilities are on the table."

Pete leaned back and smiled. "Jim, I always pegged you as a cool, even-keeled cat. But look at you. That look in your eyes is fired up. If it wasn't snowing so much outside, I'd guess you would be ready to run to that field on foot."

He looked at his coffee and chuckled. "I've spent so many years waiting for this opportunity. Looking for it. It's so close I can taste it and that makes me come alive."

The waitress returned with two short stacks of pancakes with maple syrup and a side of bacon for each of them. They thanked her while they unraveled their silverware and dug into breakfast.

"What made you get into this, Jim? You and I haven't really talked about this before. What drove you to get into paranormal activity?"

Jim took a bite of his pancakes and spoke between chewing. "I was a World War II nut as a kid. My grandfather fought in the Air Force during that war, so he used to tell me stories of fighting the Nazis and traveling all over Europe. It was always exciting to hear that stuff. I devoured any book or documentary on the war. At the library one day—I was probably twelve years old at the time, I think—I found this book on the Nazis and their obsession with the occult."

His companion shook his head while he sipped his coffee. "Of all the things for the Nazis to pay attention to in the middle of a stinking war."

"I know, right? That's what caught my attention. And hearing these horrible stories about all the experiments they put prisoners through—it would make me shudder. But I read about these guys who were in charge of researching the occult sciences."

Pete pointed at him. "Operation Alsos, right?" Operation Alsos was a US scientific intelligence initiative which uncovered documents and artifacts related to German military projects.

"Right. So they go to this bombed villa in Berlin, and they find all kinds of stuff from Heinrich Himmler's science organization."

"And Hitler gave Himmler a whole mess of money to run that." Pete nodded and took another mouthful.

"You bet. And they found all kinds of artifacts in that villa because they studied the paranormal, different religious rites, and things of that nature. They tried to see if they could tap into the occult and weaponize it. That fascinated me."

"What, weaponizing the occult?"

"Sure. Think about it. Let's say we uncover, uh...a werewolf creature. Think of your typical werewolf—big, hairy, vicious, and strong. An angry beast that can rip you limb from limb and overpower you in one-on-one combat. If the legends are true, a werewolf is impervious to bullets, too. Wouldn't you want something like that on your side?"

After swallowing a bite of pancakes, Pete shook his head. "Then he's obliterated with one silver bullet."

"Maybe. But if we learn how to breed werewolves, we can build an entire army around them and train them to fight for us. What army can afford to stock silver bullets in all their guns? Okay, that's a far-fetched idea, but you get the point. Accessing the paranormal and the supernatural, putting it to work for us...that's a really interesting idea to me."

"Did you ever take a look at our records on Alsos?"

Jim chuckled. "It was the first thing I did when I joined the CIA. And this is where I got even more passionate about it. I don't know if you ever looked at those records, but the other thing they found in that villa's basement was a bunch of ashes and a baby's skull."

"Ugh." Pete twisted his face and put his fork down. "I didn't see that."

He leaned in and lowered his head as he grimaced. "Disgusting. There's no proof that the Nazis ever accessed much of anything supernatural, but even looking for it, they did some heinous stuff. It's not only about putting the supernatural to good use. It's about making sure it doesn't fall into the wrong hands."

The other man picked his fork up again and resumed eating. "I hear what you're saying. And yeah, the supernatural can be a real asset to a military operation. Even if it's fake."

He wrinkled his forehead. "What do you mean?"

"The Aswangs?" Pete raised his eyebrows in response to his blank stare. "Come on, the US going after the Huks in the Philippines?"

His memory jogged. "Oh, right, right...the Aswangs. Some vampire creature, right?"

Pete stabbed another bite of pancake. "The Filipino soldiers were terrified of it. They thought it sucked your blood out from your neck like a vampire would. They rebelled against the US and they sent Edward Lansdale down to deal with them."

"And he made them believe there was one lurking around them."

"That was a brilliant tactic." He picked his coffee up. "Ed has a few soldiers nab one of the enemy, puncture the guy's neck, hang him upside down and drain his blood, then toss the body back on the trail. Hey presto, it looks like he was attacked by a vampire."

Jim's eyes lit up. "Now, see? Imagine if we can get a vampire on our side. Forget breeding them or anything like that. One vampire. We're in a tough situation with an enemy? Fly the vampire out, have him or her drain the blood from a captured soldier, and scare the living daylights out of the opposition. It's fantastic."

"It could save lives, too." His companion nodded. "One vampire could strike enough fear into the hearts of men that you could bring wars to a screeching halt. It'd be like dropping an atomic bomb but without killing so many people."

He leaned back and sipped on his coffee with a smile. "See, that's what I'm talking about. The occult and the supernatural can be a tool and a very effective one. It's like putting a Super Soldier on your team. Plus, we're helping the vampire, right? They want to suck blood and we'd give them an endless supply, basically. There are numerous conflicts in the world that we can deploy a vampire to."

Pete put his fork down and folded his hands in front of him. "Although…suppose we get our hands on a real vampire or werewolf or whatever it is that we discover out there. And it's only one of them. We ship that creature out to a remote battlefield somewhere, things go badly, and the creature is killed. We're back where we started, aren't we?"

After inhaling deeply through his nose, Jim folded his arms. "If that's the way we approach it, sure. But if we only have one at our disposal, we need to find a way to create more of them."

"What? Like breeding?"

He shrugged. "Maybe. We'll have to conduct some tests and determine where, biologically speaking, the creature's powers come from. If that's something we can isolate, we can maybe pass it on to someone else. We're at the beginning here. Let's first find whatever this thing is and get it into the lab."

Pete's mind drifted back to the nightmarish stories of the Nazi doctors performing their horrific tests. He thought of that baby's skull in the basement of the villa. "We're better than them, though, right?"

"Who?"

"The Nazis. I don't want us to get carried away here and start putting humans' lives at risk."

Jim waved his hand dismissively. "Nah. I wouldn't worry about it. Humans are always our first priority. Whatever we do to this creature, we'll do it in the name of science—to learn more about it. We're trying to exploit its strengths. That's a good thing. We won't force any humans to risk their lives."

The other man nodded, although he noticed Jim's focus on using the word humans when talking about safety. *He's not thinking about the creature's safety or wellbeing.*

CHAPTER THREE

Craig flipped his laptop open, eager to start another workday.

The podcast numbers had increased steadily, and he was excited to see how far he could grow his following. The blended family angle was the perfect solution he'd needed.

Not only do I see success, I really love the work. I tell you what, Carol, it amazes me that I even managed to pull this off.

His wife always said that he was talented enough to go in any direction he wanted to professionally. But whenever he felt like his job was in trouble, he stressed about it. Being laid off had forced him out of his comfort zone. Whenever he saw a new deposit in his bank account from his podcast earnings, he heard a little voice in the back of his head—Carol saying, "I told you so."

He opened his inbox and saw the usual suspects—interview requests, newsletters that he'd already forgotten he'd signed up for, a couple of bills... Halfway down the page, one subject line caught his eye: *See you in Chicago?*

I'm not planning any trips to Chicago. What is this? It must be spam. I'm surprised the filter didn't catch it.

Curious, he clicked on the email. He always found spam emails amusing but this wasn't spam at all.

Mr. Watson,

We would like to personally invite you to The Mic, a national podcast conference being held on April 22nd through April 25th!

Unlike other podcast conferences, The Mic is unique in that it is exclusive to only podcasts that have built up significant audiences. It's an opportunity unlike any other in the industry—a chance for you to network with other content creators in a fun, uplifting atmosphere.

We believe success breeds success, so our goal every year is to maximize your success by bringing together only the top podcasters in the country.

There will be special workshops, featured presenters, and social gatherings all centered around building bonds with others in the podcasting world.

Tickets for the entire weekend start at only seven hundred and ninety-five dollars.

We hope to see you there!

Craig leaned back in his chair and took a deep breath. He folded his hands and rested them on his stomach while he stared at the email in front of him.

Boy, that sounds like a great opportunity. He looked around the room. The girls were off at school. He was completely alone.

Working at home had been comforting in many respects but lately, the loneliness had worn on him. When he worked at the paper, he spent his downtime sipping coffee in the break room with fellow journalists and other people who worked there.

The thought reminded him that he needed a refill, so he stood, grabbed his mug, and walked down the hallway into the kitchen. His footsteps echoed through the house as his heels dragged across the linoleum.

He picked the pot up and poured a fresh cup. *This used to be a great time to ask Wendy about her kids or hear what Tim did last weekend.* He looked up and leaned against the countertop. *I hated the politics of the office. And the lousy coffee. But I sure do miss the friendships.*

Wendy wasn't close to him, so they immediately lost touch. Tim had texted him a few times since the layoff, but because he wasn't reachable when they took their sojourn to Austria, his former coworkers had moved on with their lives.

Maybe it's time for me to build new friendships. This conference would be a cool opportunity to do that. I could network, meet new people... It could really change my whole world.

He smiled. *Shoot, maybe there are numerous things that other podcasters do that I don't. I could be leaving all kinds of money on the table. It would help to learn more about the industry, especially from people who actually know what they're doing.*

He pushed away from the countertop and started walking down the hall, then paused to look into Vickie's room. He winced.

Ah, you can't do that. The girls won't be able to handle it on their own around here. They're only fifteen years old. Besides, how much do you trust an emotional vampire to keep things under control while you're gone? If you went and left them here, you'd be a basket case.

Craig returned to his room and sat at his desk. He stared blankly out the window. *Still, if you somehow made it work that weekend, you could really skyrocket your podcast. How great would it be if you managed to multiply your earnings? You could provide for these girls even more effectively. You could advance your career dramatically. That really could be worth the hassle and the stress.*

His mind drifted back to the weekend vacation he took with Carol before Alexis was born. They had only spent a night there, but they squeezed in time at the Museum of Science & Industry as well as an entire day at the Shedd Aquarium.

The two of them had so much fun together. He smiled as he recalled her eyes lighting up as she pet the stingray at the Aquarium. Or how excited she was to walk through the special Walt Disney exhibit at the Museum during that trip.

There's so much to do in Chicago. What if I pulled them out of school for a couple of days? I could bring them with me, set them up at the hotel with a couple of city passes, and they could go off on their own while I go to the conference.

But that idea wouldn't work either. *That's no different than leaving them alone here. Except here, they know what they're doing. Having them running around Chicago by themselves doesn't help.*

Craig sighed heavily and took another sip of coffee. He clicked the archive button on the email. *I guess it's not the right time.*

That evening, the girls cooked dinner. Vickie was really

starting to get the hang of things in the kitchen. The two of them baked pretzel-crusted tilapia, and the smell of the baked fish filled the house with a delicate, pleasing aroma.

Craig sank deeply into his recliner in the living room while the girls mashed the potatoes. *They're really doing well in the kitchen. At least I know they could cook for themselves while I was away. But forget it. That's not the issue.*

In the kitchen, the girls joked around as Vickie mashed the potatoes in the pot.

"You know, we had potatoes back home, but I never thought of eating them like this." She looked at her adopted sister.

Alexis raised her eyebrows. "How did you eat them? Baked?"

She shrugged and resumed mashing. "I guess so. We put them near the fire until they were soft. You guys do so many different things with them. If I had known French fries were a thing, I would have willingly gone into that coffin!"

The girls laughed. At times, she adopted a little gallows humor about her four-hundred-year nap.

When they were done, Alexis called her father into the kitchen. With his hands in his pockets, he shuffled in and gave the girls a polite smile before he took a seat at the table.

Alexis tilted her head and squinted at him. *Something's bothering him.* Her father was terrible at keeping his negative emotions hidden. If he was worried or depressed, he wore it on his face whether he knew it or not.

Recognizing that had become second nature to her. During the days of her mother's treatment, she often found herself trying to cheer him up and to keep him going. He never realized it and thought he had to do the same for her, especially after Carol died.

He stared out the bay window while the girls brought the food to the table. "It looks delicious, ladies." He could barely muster up a convincing tone of voice.

As they filled their plates, Vickie talked about her day, oblivious to his expression. Alexis watched her father, worried that something terrible had happened.

Finally, she spoke up. "Dad, something is wrong."

He looked up from his plate. "What is it?"

"You tell me. You're obviously worried about something."

He smiled. "Oh, am I? And how would you know that?"

She dabbed her mouth with her napkin while she chewed a mouthful of fish. "Oh, please, Dad. I can read you like a book. Is it the podcast? Are you sick? What happened today?"

Craig chuckled at his daughter's perceptiveness. *I can't hide anything from her, exactly like I couldn't hide anything from her mother.* "It's nothing that big. I'm not sick. The podcast is doing fine. I'm just... I don't know, getting lonely."

Alexis felt a twinge of nervousness. *Mom hasn't been gone for even a year and he's already lonely? I've been worried about having this conversation with him.* "What are you saying, Dad? Do you need company?"

He shrugged. "It's not that. Girls, I had an invitation to a podcast convention. It'd be really cool to go and a great opportunity, but I have to sit it out."

The girls looked at each other, confused. "Why would you do that?" Vickie wondered.

"It's, like, four days. And it's in Chicago toward the end of this month. I wouldn't leave you both for four days."

Alexis smirked. "Why not?"

"You're only fifteen! Who would keep an eye on you? What if something happened while I was gone?" He stabbed another piece of fish. "I wouldn't be able to forgive myself. I'm not leaving you two alone for half a week."

After putting her fork down beside her plate, Alexis leaned forward and rested her chin on her fists. "Dad, do you believe that Vickie and I are responsible girls?"

"Of course."

"We already have a ride to school every day, so there are no problems there. We couldn't skip or we'd get detention and you'd find out about it anyway." She began counting on her fingers as she listed the reasons for him to go. "If we were in danger of any physical harm or something, Vickie would see it coming and, you know, react appropriately. And we can cook for ourselves. You only need to make sure the fridge and cabinets are full and you can go do whatever you want."

Craig rocked in his chair. "I don't know..."

"I'm with Alexis on this one." Vickie nodded. "If you want to go somewhere and have a little fun, you deserve it. You work hard for us."

He shook his head. "It's not only about fun. It would be a cool opportunity to network with other podcasters, learn a little more about the business, and maybe grow this little income stream we've put together."

Alexis waved her hands and shook her head. "That settles it. You're going."

He folded his arms and smiled at his daughter. *She has the same spunk her mother had.* "Oh, really? And since when do you make the decisions?"

She took the last mouthful of her potatoes. "Dad, you need to do this for yourself. If this could help the business as well, why not? The only reason you're considering staying home is us. We can fend for ourselves here and it's only a few days. We'll make sure we're both off work, and we can stick around here all weekend. No parties and no drama. And half the time, we'll be in school anyway."

She's right about that.

"Besides all that, Chicago is only a couple of hours away. If there were an emergency for some reason, you could jump in the car and be home the same day. It's honestly not that big a deal."

She's selling this hard. I have to hand it to her.

He nodded reluctantly. "Okay. I'll get a ticket for myself and make arrangements. But you two have to promise you'll be on your best behavior while I'm gone."

The girls high-fived, which was little comfort to him. They were almost a little too eager.

CHAPTER FOUR

Krista and Vickie darted and zigzagged across the makeshift court set up in the main gym of the high school.

Clutching paddles in their hands, they knocked the small wiffle ball over the net against their opponents.

Sweat dripped down Krista's forehead and smudged her makeup. Vickie wasn't sweating at all but she wiped her forehead regularly as if she was so that her makeup would be smudged as well.

Gym class was often difficult for her, simply because of her proximity to other students. During cross country, she could find places out on a course where she didn't have to look like she was trying hard when no one was around.

In gym, two dozen other students were right there, along with the teacher. That meant forty-two minutes of pretending to be tired from all the running around.

That wasn't the only problem, though. She had grown competitive, and the temptation to tap into her super-speed or strength often enticed her. But she always shoved it aside in her mind and forced herself to be more average for the sake of fitting in.

That week, the class was learning about pickleball—essentially, a full-sized version of ping pong played with small wiffle balls and teams of two. Because Krista was in her class, Vickie felt comfortable playing with her as much as she could. Much like the others in the class, the friends stuck together.

Their opponents on that particular day were Shelly and Abby. Shelly was a short redheaded girl who rarely interacted with Vickie but seemed nice enough.

Abby, however, was one of Megan Fitz's best friends. As such, she never took kindly to the vampire. The girl was over six feet tall with long dark hair that fell halfway down her back. Her perfectly sculpted eyebrows often appeared to be angry by default, and she usually pursed her lips in a somewhat cocky expression.

Despite her size, Abby wasn't much of an athlete. She huffed and puffed as the two distance runners on the other side of the net darted skillfully and lobbed the ball over the net. Shelly played soccer and had some endurance, but her partner was the weak link.

Because Vickie sensed this and wanted to win the match, she repeatedly sent the ball over the net on Abby's side. Part of her enjoyed watching the girl get visibly frustrated at having to return it so often.

Abby's face became flushed, and her dark hair stuck to her forehead. Before the match, she had scowled at the vampire, confident that she and Shelly would wipe the floor with them. But that didn't happen.

Vickie served the wiffle ball one last time and dropped it barely over the net so Abby had to launch herself forward and almost dive to return the shot. She landed on her stomach, but her paddle missed the ball, which bounced off the floor twice and gave Krista and Vickie the winning point.

Shelly shook her head but politely congratulated them both. "Nice game."

The two girls on the other side walked forward and high-fived her. Abby pulled herself into a sitting position on the gym floor and sneered at Vickie. Shelly offered a hand to help her up, but she ignored it.

When all the matches were over, Mr. Kolander, the gym class teacher that day, gathered the students.

"Okay, everyone, it looks like we have our winners for Pickleball Week. Congratulations to Bill and Curtis for the guys, and on the girls' side, our champions are Krista and Vickie."

The class applauded politely for the two winning teams —except for Abby, of course.

"Nice hustle today, class. You have about twenty minutes before the period is over. I'll give you a little extra time today because I see many of you are sweaty and I want you to have a chance to use the showers if you need it."

The boys and girls returned to their respective locker rooms.

Krista grimaced as she wiped her forehead again. "I can't stop sweating. Ugh. I'll need to rinse my face off, at least, and freshen up."

"Oh, yeah, me too." Vickie lied often, but it was easier to simply follow along than stand out.

The two girls walked over to the sinks in the locker rooms, turned on the faucets, and doused their faces with cold water to cool themselves off.

"Ahhhhh, much better." Krista smiled into the mirror as she let the water drip off her face. "Like twenty minutes is enough time for a girl to take a shower anyway."

Vickie nodded and looked at her now makeup-free face in the mirror as well. "Yeah. At least this takes care of the basics."

They toweled their faces and heads, then walked over to their lockers to change. While they were getting dressed, Krista chuckled. "Oh, boy, you better get some makeup on."

"What is it?" The vampire touched her face with her fingertips, curious as to what was wrong.

"You have a huge zit on the end of your nose!"

"I do?" Vickie touched her nose and felt a bump. She finished getting dressed and walked over to the mirror. Sure enough, a large red zit lurked noticeably at the end of her nose. "Oh, look at that. I hope it goes away soon."

Krista nodded. "Zits don't last too long for me either. But that's a big one. Don't leave this locker room without covering it up."

Abby leaned against her locker and watched this unfold. With a devilish grin, she slipped her phone out of her pocket. Her father had bought her the latest high-end Android phone, complete with high-definition zoom.

Pretending that she was checking her Snapchat or something, she lifted the phone and discreetly zoomed in on Vickie in the mirror. With a quick tap, she snapped a photo of the vampire's face before she covered her zit with makeup.

Once the picture was taken and Vickie began to cover the offending blemish, Abby sat and held her phone closely to double-check the result.

Oh, man, this is good. I can't wait to show Megan. Those fluorescent lights surrounding the mirror really highlight that thing!

While her mind raced with ideas of what to do with it, she texted the picture to Megan, who was in world history at the time.

Despite the school policy against it, Megan kept her phone in her pocket and felt it vibrate. Because she sat at the back of the classroom and Mr. Lehninger was an older teacher, she could pull her phone out and look at the message without being seen.

She snorted when she saw the picture and texted Abby immediately.

Megan: *OMG look at that thing*

Abby: *Hilarious right?*

Megan: *You have to do something with this!*

Abby: *Like what?*

Abby: *Blackmail? Print up posters?*

Megan: *Tag her on FB*

Abby: *lol I should*

Megan: *You totally should. Do it tonight*

Abby: *She'll be mad*

Megan: *So what? She can't do anything to you*

As the makeup covered up the zit on her face, Vickie smiled at Krista. "Thanks for pointing that one out. I probably would have walked right out of here without even noticing."

That wasn't a lie. She honestly didn't understand what the big deal was about zits. She had seen it when she washed her face but it didn't occur to her that she would need to cover it.

Krista smiled and patted her on the back. "No sweat. At least nobody really saw it in here. Everyone's too worried about themselves. That's why we wear makeup."

They carried their makeup bags to their lockers. Vickie sensed that Abby was watching her and flashed her a confused look.

The girl merely smiled at her. "Good game today."

"Oh, thanks." She nodded politely, a little confused as to why she was being nice to her. "You too. Maybe next time, you'll win."

"Maybe next time." Abby gave her an insincere smile. "Or maybe sooner than that." She grabbed her backpack and headed to the door, where other students were waiting for the bell to ring.

"What was that about?" Krista asked as she zipped her backpack and slung it over her shoulder.

"I don't know." Vickie slammed her locker shut. "I feel like Megan and her friends spend all their free time trying to think of ways to get at me."

Her friend nodded while she pulled her hair into a ponytail. "Some people have nothing better to do, I guess. But who cares? It's not like you did anything today. She has nothing. Those girls probably want to play mind games with you. They're bullies, pure and simple."

The bell rang and the girls nodded to one another as

they went separate ways down the hall. Abby followed Vickie at a distance. She needed to go in the same direction but didn't want to walk anywhere near her.

Just wait until tonight. It'll be great and when everyone is home, sitting on Facebook, you'll totally look ridiculous.

CHAPTER FIVE

Alexis paced in the school hallway and peered impatiently down the long corridor. *Come on, let's go. I want to go home.*

Finally, at the end of the hall, Vickie and Eric appeared, walking hand-in-hand and bumping into each other playfully as they giggled. She rolled her eyes at the sight, then returned to leaning up against the bank of lockers where she had paced a few moments before.

They both smiled as they approached her. She nodded to them. "About time."

Surprised by her tone, Vickie drew her eyebrows together. "Is everything okay?"

She shrugged. "It's fine. I…let's get going. Our ride will leave if we don't get out to the parking lot."

The vampire gave her a warm smile. "Sure. I only have to grab a few things."

Eric slid over beside Alexis while Vickie opened her locker and dropped her backpack on the floor. She unzipped it and pulled out a few books that she tossed into the bottom of her locker.

"Do you have much homework tonight?" Eric asked politely.

"Nope." Alexis stared forward and didn't make any eye contact with him.

He picked up on her tone but didn't want to ask in front of Vickie. Instead, he nodded awkwardly and returned his attention to his girlfriend.

Vickie straightened, satisfied with the books she packed, and slipped her arm through the strap of her backpack. She tilted her locker door open a little more so she could admire the photo of Eric she had taped to the inside.

Her boyfriend chuckled and nudged her. "Who's that goofy-looking guy?" he joked.

"Oh, I think he's handsome, actually." She wound her arms around his neck and pulled him in for a sweet little kiss.

Meanwhile, Alexis bounced the back of her head off the locker door and continued to stare ahead. *Gosh, these two are the worst. Do they have to lay it on so thick all the time? I miss when Eric was simply a friend, not some schmoopy boyfriend.* "Whenever you're ready."

"She's right, I gotta go." Vickie slammed her locker door and gave Eric one more kiss. "I'll talk to you tonight, okay?"

The girls walked down a short set of stairs and through the door to the parking lot. The sunshine reflecting off the snow was blinding, and as it melted, the sound of water splashing into the sewer drain was equally as distracting.

"Boy, it's not as peaceful out here as it was even last

week!" Vickie shook her head in disbelief. "How quickly the weather changes here."

Alexis said nothing.

"I bet there won't be any snow left on this parking lot by Monday."

Once again, she received no response.

She must be tired from a long class or something and obviously not in the mood to talk. But after they climbed into the car and got on the road headed home, Vickie started to catch a sense of what was going on.

Alexis sat in the front seat, staring out the window, while she sat behind her and stared at her sister in an attempt to understand the situation. *She's not hurt and doesn't seem to be unhealthy or uncomfortable. This is pure emotion. I can sense it.*

The vampire quietly took a few deep breaths while she sank deeper into the vibe that Alexis gave off. *Something is bothering her emotionally. She's trying to bury it deep inside her, but it's still there, eating away at her. Too bad I can't pinpoint what the problem actually is.*

She resolved to give Alexis some time to cool off rather than badger her with questions. She'd learned fairly quickly in America about people not being in the mood to talk. While she didn't understand the concept, she respected it.

They reached the house and climbed out of the car, lugging their backpacks behind them. Alexis walked on ahead and tried to turn the doorknob, but it was locked. She scowled, then yanked her keys from her pocket.

Vickie walked up behind her. "Is it locked?"

"Yep."

"That's weird. Your dad doesn't usually go anywhere during the day."

"Nope."

Well, I got a few words out of her anyway. She followed the girl into the house once the door was unlocked. "Hello?"

They received no answer. Craig was not at home.

When Alexis walked past the counter, she saw a small yellow Post-It note stuck to the laminate, its bottom corners rolled up and practically waving the girls over to read it.

She got there first, read the note, and walked away, shaking her head.

Confused, Vickie leaned over to read the note, which was very short:

> *Shopping for the trip. Be back by dinner. Love you!*
> *P.S. Can you run the vacuum through, please?*

Vickie looked down the hall in time to see Alexis close the door behind her. She didn't slam it but didn't ease it into the frame, either. She cocked an eyebrow. *Is she going to vacuum, or is she assuming that I will do it?*

She walked to her bedroom and dropped her backpack, then knocked on Alexis' door.

"What?"

"Let me in."

"Why?"

"We have chores to do."

Alexis groaned and stood from her bed. She opened the door and let Vickie in. Without a word, she turned her back on her and walked back to the bed.

"Your dad wants us to vacuum."

"Yeah, I read it."

The vampire tilted her head in confusion. "Okay, so… who's doing it?"

Her sister stared at the phone in her hands. "I don't feel like it."

She folded her arms. "What's your deal right now? You've been crabby ever since we left school."

"I'm fine." She still didn't look up from her phone. "Whatever. I'll vacuum."

"No, don't worry about it." Vickie held her palm out. "I'll take care of it. I'll do it quicker anyway. Just…cool off in here." She walked out and closed the door behind her.

She's irritated with me about something. That much I can sense. But what did I do? She was fine this morning. It had to have happened either at the end of the day or near the end of the day. That's when she was bothered by me.

Shaking her head, Vickie opened the closet door at the front of the house where the vacuum cleaner was stored. She pulled it out and plugged it in and began to take long, deep breaths to warm up.

Don't move too fast or you'll make mistakes. Or you'll leave dirt behind. You have to only move fast enough that the vacuum can catch most of it and don't run into anything.

She placed her right hand on the handle and closed her eyes. Her blood began to flow and quickly filled her body with energy and adrenaline.

When she felt sufficiently energized, she pressed the switch on the vacuum and it roared to life. She moved rapidly from room to room and vacuumed at super-speed. It was a jarring experience as she could move very quickly but had to stop repeatedly to prevent herself from running through a wall or pounding a hole into a closet door.

Still, a job that normally took about half an hour only took about twenty seconds, although she skipped Alexis's room. *We'll vacuum that next time.*

Vickie returned to the front of the house and began to coil the vacuum cord when Alexis emerged and walked past the entrance to the living room on her way to the kitchen for a snack.

Once she put the appliance back in the closet, the vampire walked to the kitchen doorway and stood with her hands in her pockets, waiting for the other girl to talk to her.

"What?"

"You're mad at me for something."

"No, I'm not."

She ran her fingers through her hair. "We both know that I can sense this kind of thing. What is the problem? Did I do something? Did I not do something? I don't like you being mad at me so please talk."

Alexis rolled her eyes while she pulled a bag of chips out of the cupboard. She knew Vickie was right but didn't want to deal with it. The girl usually meant well, so this wasn't something that was done on purpose.

But still, it bothered her.

"Look, you clearly knew that Will was a Sang. You knew that he…consumed human flesh. And yet you didn't tell me? And you let him take me out alone? Several times?"

The vampire was taken completely by surprise. "Alexis, that was months ago. Has it bothered you for this long?"

Her sister opened the bag of chips, placed the chip clip

on the countertop, and dug for a handful. "Not all the time. But…well, watching you and Eric is a reminder to me that I had a boyfriend too. Or I thought I did. Whatever that was, I hung out with someone who wanted to bite my neck and drain the blood from my body. I was in immense danger, and you didn't tell me."

Vickie shook her head. "I fought Will for you. I'm the reason he's gone now."

"But you put me at risk. And for what? What was worth risking my life?"

She exhaled sharply through her nose, frustrated. "Will hated me, not you. He called me his enemy. I thought he would attack me. We even fought a couple of times. And you were so happy to have a boyfriend, I didn't want to ruin that."

"I'd rather you ruin it like that than let it be ruined by attempted murder." Alexis pulled a soda out of the fridge. "I'll be fine. I only…I don't know why you didn't tell me. I couldn't protect myself, and I spent time alone with him. I should be dead by now."

The girl pushed past her, walked down the hallway, and slammed her bedroom door shut this time. Vickie turned and looked out the patio door at the open field behind the house. *If you only knew what I went through to try to keep you safe, Alexis. If you only knew.*

She walked to the middle bedroom and slammed her door shut as well, leaving a completely quiet house while the girls avoided each other.

CHAPTER SIX

D inner was a quiet affair that evening.

Craig had returned home from the store, jazzed about his pending trip to Chicago. He even ordered a pizza delivery for the family since he had spent considerable time at the store and didn't mind springing for something a little more special.

He tore off a slice for himself and plopped it excitedly on his plate. With a smile on his face, he cracked his can of soda open and looked at the girls, who were both expressionless as they selected slices for themselves.

"That's it?" He shrugged at them. "Come on. I even sprung for the good takeout pizza tonight. Is nobody else excited?"

Vickie smiled politely at him. "I'm sure it'll be delicious. Thanks."

"Yeah, thanks, Dad."

They both stared at their plates while he looked at them, slack-jawed. *Geez, I didn't expect them to throw me a parade or anything, but I thought they'd be a little more excited than this.*

He bit into his slice and stretched the mozzarella cheese from his lips to his fingers before he bit it off. "How was school today?"

"Fine."

"It was okay."

Craig took a sip of his soda to wash the pizza down and watched the two of them. Vickie was eating but kept her head down. Alexis pushed her slice of pizza around on her plate and took an occasional nibble or sip of soda.

It was hardly the enthusiastic dinner he had hoped for.

His mind wandered as he took another bite. *Hey, you don't know that much about girls. Maybe this is simply a teenage girl thing. Their hormones are all over the place. Maybe they've simply bottomed out tonight. Don't push it. The last thing you want to do is set them off.*

"I picked up some of the good ice cream while I was out, too." He received no response. "I emailed the organizer of the convention. I guess they're expecting a few famous celebrities with podcasts, too. Joe Rogan will be there, and those funny guys from the one where they review bad movies. I forget their names. But hey, I'll get to rub shoulders with some bigwigs."

"It sounds cool, Dad." Alexis couldn't have sounded less impressed if she'd tried.

The remainder of the dinner was silent as he finally gave up trying to maintain a conversation. He enjoyed the pizza, at least.

But the girls remained silent. They hadn't really fought

like this before, and they were both angry at each other for how they felt.

After dinner, they went to their rooms. Craig was too excited about his trip, so he stayed up and watched an old movie to calm his mind. *I won't be able to sleep if I'm this excited.*

Halfway through the movie, he fell asleep in his chair, his hands folded on his stomach. His eyes snapped open as the credits rolled.

He stood and walked to the kitchen to get a drink of water. On the way, he paused at the microwave to check the time. *1:30 a.m. Oof. I'll be tired in the morning.*

After getting his drink, he peered down the hall to make sure the girls' bedroom lights were off. They were, so he went to sleep.

The next morning, he rolled over in bed and checked the time. The sunlight streamed through the window, very gradually melting the snow and making everything outside a wet, muddy mess.

Oh, it's after 6:30 a.m. already. I'd better get up and wish the girls a good day before they leave.

To his surprise, however, only Alexis sat at the kitchen table, eating a bowl of Cap'n Crunch. "Morning, Dad."

"Morning, kid." He rubbed his eyes. "Where's Vickie?"

She shrugged and didn't look up. "Probably still in bed."

"Seriously? You have to leave in, like, two minutes."

She smirked when she heard the car roll into the driveway. "Sooner than that, I bet." She stood and pushed her chair in before she carried her bowl to the sink.

Craig rushed into the vampire's room and turned the

light on. A groggy Vickie rolled over and opened her eyes. "What?"

"Your ride is here. You'll be late for school. Get up!"

She stretched and yawned. "It's okay. Tell them to go. I'll catch up."

He hesitated, then walked to the door and waved for them to go. *I hope you know what you're doing.* He closed the inside door and walked through the kitchen in time to see her emerge from her room and head to the bathroom. *Okay, at least she's up.* "Will you need a ride?"

"No, don't worry about it."

Whatever. He sat in his recliner and retrieved his tablet. *As if teenage girls weren't confusing enough. Vampire teenage girls are so much worse.*

He put his feet up and opened his news app to scan the headlines for the day. Vickie walked past him, fully-dressed.

"What's your plan, girl?"

She shuffled in. "I'll eat a quick breakfast, then speed my way through."

"You're going to run to school? Are you nuts? You'll be outed in seconds." He pointed to the sidewalk. "The students at that middle school down the street will see you coming out of the house and that will be it."

The vampire giggled. "No, it won't. I'll start moving in here. If you don't mind closing the door behind me so I don't accidentally pull it off its hinges…"

"Fine. Are you sure this will work? I know you can run, but—"

She waved her hand dismissively. "No sweat. I can't be seen by the naked eye anyway when I run. If I'm invisible when I run, I simply start running in here and I'll already be invisible before I set foot outside."

It wasn't the worst plan, in his mind. She had clearly thought it through and wasn't like he could stop her if he tried.

He returned to the news as Vickie hurtled through the house. The curtains on the windows billowed every time she rushed past. Within a few seconds, she had made her bed, packed her backpack, done her hair, and was ready for the day.

She stopped rushing only to eat breakfast because she didn't want to risk damaging any dishes.

Finally, she was ready to go, and she swung by the living room again to say goodbye.

"Have a good day," Craig said warmly to her. "Are you sure you don't want a ride?"

Vickie smiled. "I'll be fine. A ride would only slow me down." On her way out the door, she stopped at a cupboard and pulled out an energy bar to consume afterward.

Without warning, she was gone. He saw her blur effortlessly to the street but lost track of her almost immediately.

She would duck, dodge, and dive on her way to school and do her absolute best not to accidentally bump into anyone and blow her cover.

Craig returned to reading but after a short while, he looked up, distracted by an odd smell in the house. He sniffed a few times but couldn't quite place what it was or where it came from.

He tried his best to continue reading, but the smell grew stronger. Finally, he stood and walked down the hall in an attempt to locate the source. He found nothing there.

The living room was also a pointless exploration but when he reached the kitchen, the smell grew even stronger.

To his shock, smoke emanated from the side door. On closer inspection, he saw a burn mark a few inches long on the wood door frame. The timber had smoldered, not actually ignited, but still, there was something close to a fire in the house.

After he doused it with a little water, he thought about how it could have happened. Then he realized that Vickie was only now taking control of her powers. *If the bottom of her shoe caught this old, dry wood frame, it could have enough friction to light it, kinda like a match.*

He smiled when he considered this is one of Vickie's least expensive things to worry about. It wasn't that big a deal. Still, he wondered if leaving town was the right call.

If I leave the city and she accidentally does this again, would Alexis be around to make sure the house doesn't burn down? Would she do this, or would she ignore it? Or even worse, what if she laughed at it?

His ticket to the conference was already paid for, so he wasn't able to stay at home for any length of time. Craig worried about money almost constantly, so he had no desire to waste that ticket.

He would go to that conference, whether he wanted to or not at this point. He merely had to make sure they were getting along and wouldn't do any serious damage to the house.

But like any good Dad, he struggled with the decision.

CHAPTER SEVEN

Craig wiped the sweat from his brow while he ran the sponge along the linoleum floor in the kitchen.

"I don't know how your mother did this every week." He grunted as he pushed himself up onto his knees. "She used to get up on Saturday mornings at, like, six a.m. and have it clean before anyone even woke up. The woman was a machine."

He looked out the window at what was left of the snow in the back yard, dreaming of jumping head-first into it to cool himself off.

"Mom didn't seem to mind cleaning." Alexis sprayed window cleaner on the patio door and began to scrub it with a rag. "I never saw her with a scowl on her face or anything when she cleaned. It's like she used it as her zen moment."

He smiled warmly. "I wouldn't put it past her. She really knew how to make the most of a lousy situation."

His daughter stepped back and squinted at the glass, making sure she had wiped all the fingerprints away. "Hey, speaking of lousy situations, why don't we do this when Vickie is around?"

The vampire was working a shift at Al's Seafood that morning.

"Look, we have to use Saturdays as the cleaning days. Sundays are for relaxing and preparing for the week, and the rest of the week is too busy. When we have a Saturday when you're working and she's not, she'll be in your place."

"What if we're both working?" She smiled.

Her father placed his hands on his hips and stared at the half-clean linoleum. "Then I'll have to get started at six a.m. if I want it done by dinnertime." They both laughed.

"It feels unfair." The glass squeaked as Alexis rubbed the rag on it.

This is as good a time as any to ask her but tread carefully. "Hey, so what is up with you two?"

"What do you mean?" Alexis didn't look at him.

"I don't know but I get a weird vibe from you both. Like, maybe you're fighting or something. No one's talking to each other, everyone's tense… I don't like living in that kind of a house. We don't do drama."

We don't do drama was a mantra Carol had repeated ad nauseum whenever she was around her family.

"Okay, Mom." Her voice dripped with sarcasm. "Where did she even come up with that?"

Craig dropped to his hands and knees again and resumed scrubbing. "Actually, the original phrase was 'I don't do drama.' She said that to me on our first date. We both had come from different overdramatic high school relationships. By the time we got together, she was over all the melodramatic problems that high schoolers have. No offense."

"Pfff."

"Anyway, once we got married, it turned into 'we don't do drama.' She liked to say it to remind ourselves that there's enough drama in life already and we don't need to add to it."

Alexis tossed the rag on the kitchen table and picked up her bottle of water. "There's no drama, Dad. Don't worry about it. We're sisters now and sometimes, we'll fight. It comes with the territory."

He nodded. "I did have numerous fights with my brothers when I was your age. Still, is there something I can help with?"

"Not at the moment." She put the water down and snatched the rag up to start washing the bay window. "I'll let you know."

"I love you both, you know that. I only want everyone to get along." The rough side of the sponge scraped the crevices of the linoleum and loosened bits of dirt.

"Hey, if you want us to get along, make her do all the cleaning!"

Craig laughed. "That wouldn't be very fair."

"Oh, please." She turned to face him. "We bust our backs for hours doing this, and she could clean the whole house in, like, five minutes. You should've seen how quickly she vacuumed the other day."

He rolled into a seated position on the floor. "What do you mean?"

Alexis turned back to the window as she tried to think

about how to explain it. She knew that she had been a jerk to Vickie and basically forced her to do the vacuuming.

"She offered to do it the other day when you left that note." She decided that was enough of an explanation without exactly lying about it. "She tapped into her super-speed and knocked it out. Seriously, Dad, it was done in, like, seconds."

Craig winced at the thought. "Yeah, but that comes with its own risks."

"Oh yeah." She rolled her eyes. "Like more free time, a cleaner house…real risky, Dad."

"That's not what I mean." He shook his head. "I'm fine with her using her speed outside. That's easy enough. There's more than enough space for her to run around and get whatever done that she needs to. But inside is a different story. If she makes one wrong move, she could do real damage to this place. Remember when she broke the side door? Or all that damage she did to the AirBNB in Austria?"

Alexis adjusted the headband that kept her hair away from her face. "She did fine, Dad. She didn't run into anything. Actually, even though I was mad at her, I was still impressed."

"It only takes one wrong move." He sighed. "One slip-up, one distraction, and we could have a huge disaster on our hands."

She shrugged. "But she has that super-awareness too. She's basically competent. I'm sure she uses that while she's on speed, or however you want to put it."

Craig laughed at his daughter's choice of words, then

pulled himself to his feet. "Come here, I want to show you something."

Curious, she followed him to the side door. He pulled it open and pointed to the threshold of the door frame at the bottom of the doorway. "Do you see that spot there?"

Alexis crouched and ran her finger along the large burned area on the wood. "Yeah, it looks like someone set this thing on fire."

He shook his head. "Nope. That was Vickie running late for school."

"How did this happen?"

"If I had to guess, I would say her shoe caught the threshold on her way out of the house. The friction from it caused a little heat to develop."

Guilt washed over her. *I was the reason she ran late that day. I didn't wake her. This is kinda my fault.* "That's one accident, Dad."

"Right, but all it takes is one accident, my dear. We're lucky that the wood only smoldered and didn't burn the whole house down. This is serious business."

She straightened again and placed her foot over the mark to measure it. Sure enough, it was about the size of her foot. She could see how that might have happened. "But maybe we tell her to pull back a tad. Tell her to watch herself more carefully or these kinds of disasters can happen. Even if she cleaned the whole house in ten minutes instead of five—"

Craig closed his eyes and pinched the bridge of his nose. "That's another thing we need to talk about." He walked across the floor and sat down at the kitchen table.

Alexis followed suit. "We can't make her do all the work for us."

"Why not?" She was genuinely confused by this idea. "If she can do it all in a few minutes without breaking a sweat, why would we give up that resource? It's perfect."

He pursed his lips. "Because she's not our slave. She's a member of the family. Vickie will share the responsibilities, of course. But we can't put her to work all the time."

Alexis twisted her face in confusion. "I'm not trying to be a jerk about it, Dad, but she can literally do everything in a few minutes. Why wouldn't we take advantage of that? Like, it's much quicker for you to clean the gutters out than for me to do it, so you do it, right? Same deal. You're better suited for it."

Craig pulled his foot up and rested it on his knee. "And you're simply trying to get out of doing the work like any good teenager would. I'm onto you. Besides the fear that a wrong move will result in my house burning down, we can't treat her like that's all she's good for."

"I'm not saying that."

"I know you're not. But that's what it would look like. We share this house—share the fun but also the chores. If we keep using Vickie's powers every time we're in a jam, we're exploiting her. That's not cool."

"I guess you're right." She shook her head. "Still...it'd be nice."

"Of course it would. We don't really know how this affects her, either. I don't think she does. Maybe she's fine using her powers whenever she wants. But I'm inclined to think that there's some kind of drawback to it. I don't know what that is, but I'm watching her closely. I don't want her to get hurt or drained of her powers because she uses them to do housework or whatever. Now, let's finish this up."

They both returned to their cleaning tasks. On his way across the kitchen, Craig turned the radio on. Classic 1990s hip-hop was playing.

"The Beastie Boys, Dad?" Alexis groaned. "Really? Act your age."

"Hey, I was your age when these guys were on fire. Have some respect for the classics, girl."

CHAPTER EIGHT

Vickie walked out of the back door of the seafood restaurant into the crisp spring evening. She bid Patti, one of her coworkers, a good night before she climbed into the SUV waiting for her.

"Whoa!" Craig almost shouted as she shut the door. He reached frantically for the buttons to roll the windows down.

"Hey, what are you doing?" Vickie tried to roll the windows up, but he locked the buttons. "Come on, it's cold out and I'm all sweaty."

"Sweat is the least of your concerns right now." He winced as he leaned his head out the window while he backed the SUV out of the parking space.

"What is your problem?" She drew her eyebrows together and shook her head at his sudden ridiculous behavior.

"You honestly don't smell that?" He looked at her, incredulous. "You reek."

She lifted the shoulder of her tan work shirt emblazoned with the Al's Seafood logo and held it to her nose before she shrugged. "I guess it smells a little fishy—"

"A little?" He laughed. "Holy cow, you must be really used to that smell. Oof. You'd better hurry up and turn sixteen so that you can drive yourself to work."

Vickie folded her arms. "Technically, I'm like four hundred years old."

"You know what I mean. What did you do at work today? My goodness, you've smelled fishy after every shift, but this is a new one."

"I worked in the back, mostly. I'm still the new person there, so I get most of the low-level stuff. They banish me to the dishwashing room much of the time."

Craig shook his head in disbelief. "How do you smell that bad doing dishes? You've done dishes before, but you haven't smelled like this."

"They do more than wash dishes back there. Any time there was a job that needed to be done in that room, they passed it to me. I had to chop up a few catfish, or they'd run out of cod that needed breading and they asked me to do it. It was a busy night."

"We should've started you on a paper route." He muttered under his breath while he tried to keep his nose out of the car, preferring to freeze his skin than breathe the fishy air.

When they got home, she walked past Alexis, who sat at the kitchen table. "Hey."

"Hey." Her sister didn't look up at first, but her face twisted as soon as she caught a whiff of Vickie's clothes. "Holy cow—"

"Yeah, yeah, I know. I'm taking a shower."

"Go ahead and burn those clothes when you're done too, please."

She walked into her room, collected a change of clothes, and headed to the bathroom. After she'd turned on the shower to let it warm up, she peeled her clothes off and took a good, long sniff. *Maybe they're right. This does totally stink.*

As she showered and scrubbed away the stench, her phone on her dresser in her bedroom—still on silent from work—glowed briefly with new text notifications from Eric. Because she was in the shower, she had no clue.

Once she'd washed and dried off, Vickie pulled on a pair of comfy shorts and a t-shirt and exited the bathroom, her stinky clothes balled up in her right arm. *Wow, now I can really smell these. Yikes.*

She tossed them into the hamper in her room, pulled her phone off her dresser, and walked down the hall without actually looking at the device.

Vickie stepped in front of Craig, who sat in his recliner in the living room. She held her arms outstretched. "Is that better now?" Her voice betrayed a slight hint of sarcasm.

Craig took a big sniff. "Much better. Thank you."

"I'm so glad I can please you all." She plopped on the couch and put her feet up, sighing with relief as she closed her eyes for a moment and took deep breaths to decompress after a few long hours of work.

All the while, Eric continued to try to text her. Her phone was still on silent.

"Long day?" Craig asked with a smirk.

Vickie didn't open her eyes. "Geez, you could've asked

me that in the car instead of complaining about my stink the whole time."

He uttered a belly laugh. "Oh, come on. There's no way you can defend that funk. It was brutal. Now that I can breathe around you again, I'm interested in talking to you. You said it was busy."

Vickie shrugged. "There seemed to be more customers than usual. I don't really know how much is called busy. Everyone acted like we were slammed, and there was a long line of customers weaving throughout the store. I worked almost the whole time without any breaks— on my feet, running around constantly. It felt like every time I would get into a groove of washing dishes, they'd have another fish for me to cut up or something."

Craig looked up from his tablet. "You didn't use your powers, did you? I'm sure speed and strength come in handy in situations like that, but—"

She waved her hand to brush the idea aside. "The dishwashing room has this huge plate glass window on the front of it looking out at the store. Everyone who came in could see any move I made. There was no chance to use my powers."

"Well, that's good." He nodded, satisfied. "I really don't want you using that stuff for frivolous jobs."

"Frivolous?"

"That simply means using it when it's not necessary. If you're in a situation where a normal human would reasonably be able to do the job without powers, you should probably stick to not using them."

Vickie sighed and tossed the phone—still unseen—on

the couch beside her. "I really wanted to today. You don't know how hard it is to have powers and not use them."

"Really?" He hadn't thought of this before.

"Oh, yeah. It takes a whole different kind of control. My instinct is to use them. If I'm inconvenienced, my body knows it can overcome the problem with the powers I have. It craves the chance to use them. Not being able to makes me anxious."

He laughed while he stretched for his glass of water on the end table. "I guess it's like putting a toddler in front of a plate of cookies and telling him not to eat them. The temptation is too strong." He took a sip. "Well, I'm glad you didn't give in. Now that you have more control over them, it's important to be very intentional about when and where you use them instead of simply whenever you feel like it."

She nodded and turned to her phone to see fourteen text messages from Eric. *What on Earth?*

As she read them, she caught the gist quickly. Apparently, pictures were being circulated on Facebook of her covering her big zit in the gym class locker room. She, however, failed to see the problem.

Doesn't everybody get zits? It seems like a dumb thing to be self-conscious about. She texted Eric a similar statement. He couldn't believe it.

Eric: *Abby did it*

Vickie: *Ok*

Eric: *They're going to be merciless*

Vickie: *Who?*

Eric: *Everyone*

Vickie: *What for? So I had a zit*

Eric: *I wish it were that easy. Maybe it's not a big deal in your country. But in American high school, anything embarrassing comes back to haunt you*

Vickie: *That's stupid*

Eric: *True*

Eric: *Check out FB*

Confused by this entire situation, she opened the Facebook app on her phone. The top post in her feed was a zoomed-in photo of her face in the locker room, posted by Abby.

Sure enough, there were already thirty-seven comments on the photo and more were being posted every minute.

The comments ranged from the sympathetic—*Oh, that's embarrassing*—to the angry—*Serves her right. Walks around like she owns the school or something*—to the cruel—*She looks like she's ready to lead Santa's reindeer into a blizzard.*

Vickie looked at the photo once again. She still didn't quite understand what all the attention was for. *I have a huge red mark on my nose. Like, that's it. It's simply a skin blemish, and I covered it with makeup right after that. Besides, this was a private moment. Everyone looks bad in private, right?*

She tapped the *Comment* button and typed in a defense:

All of you are being really mean for no reason. I had a zit. Who cares? Doesn't everyone get zits from time to time? Besides, is no one going to mention the fact that this was taken in private? I shouldn't have to hide in the locker room. All girls wear makeup. This is stupid.

Within seconds, Megan Fitz commented: *Easy, Rudolph.*

Once he saw the comment, Eric picked his phone up and called her. "Vickie, you should probably delete that comment you posted."

"What for?" Now, she was getting frustrated. "Why are there so many unwritten rules to being a teenager that I need to know about? Can't I simply be me?"

"I think it's fine. I really do." He wanted her to feel comfortable in her own skin but not careless with her reputation. "It is only a zit. But the second you let people know that you're bothered by this, they'll pounce on you like a shark on a swimmer with a broken leg."

Vickie stood, walked to her bedroom, and closed the door behind her. "Eric, I'm tired. I've had a long day. I wanted to relax and now, I have all these comments about a photo of me that shouldn't have been shared. It's not even that bad. But now that I defend myself, I'm making it worse? I should simply sit here and let people make fun of me?"

Eric had no words of comfort. He knew he was right, but he also knew that this was frustrating for her. The picture didn't bother him. He loved that it didn't bother her. But because she was not from America, he didn't want her oblivious mistakes in handling this to make the situation worse.

"Try not to engage anyone on it. Ignore it. Move on. Don't get sucked into this mess. That's what they want you to do. I bet Megan was waiting for you to reply so that she could call you Rudolph."

After a few minutes of chatting—during which Eric tried his best to change the subject and keep her from dwelling on it—she hung up and then opened the Facebook app again.

The post was still at the top. In the comments, Abby

posted a response with a Photoshopped version of the picture, adding a large clown nose instead.

So stupid. Apparently, no one has anything to do with their time anymore. She closed the app and threw herself on her bed to stare at the ceiling. *This kind of thing never happened back home, that's for sure.*

CHAPTER NINE

Vickie strolled through the back door of Al's Seafood, whistling quietly. She enjoyed walking into work with a fresh work shirt—one that didn't yet smell like fish —and felt clean, good, and ready to make money.

"Whoa." She stopped in her tracks as she passed the walk-in cooler to the back storage area. The path through the room she normally took to reach the punch clock was blocked by stacks and stacks of massive boxes.

"Move them out of the way so you can punch in!" Her boss, Jason, shouted from the dishwashing room.

To her surprise, the boxes were actually quite light, even without her strength powers. "Huh." She was amused by this as she slid them aside and blazed a new path to the clock.

After punching in, she turned to see Jason, a diminutive man with thinning, long brown hair peeking out from his official black Al's Seafood baseball hat. He was retying his apron as he greeted her.

"What's with all the boxes?" She tapped one of them, which echoed. "They sound empty."

"These are rolls." He walked over to one and ripped it open to reveal dozens of packages of freshly baked rolls.

"What's the occasion?" Vickie knew there was no way the manager would order this many rolls without reason. They would pick up mold before they could be sold.

"We are entering the busiest season of the year—Lent." He clapped his hands as she gave him a confused look. "Yeah, I know, it's a little late this year, but I don't make the calendars."

"No, what's Lent?"

"Lent is a time when many people who go to church swear off eating meat. Usually Catholics, but there are others too. Regardless, seafood places are always inundated. Here in Wisconsin, you already have the Friday Fish Fry crowd and now, there are thousands of people who aren't eating meat and need to get their fix. So they eat fish and tons of it. We go through a huge number of orders, and many people eat sandwiches. That's why we've loaded up on rolls."

Vickie nodded. The answer was good enough for her. The rolls smelled delicious, though, and she was a sucker for a nice, soft piece of bread. "I don't get to eat these, then?" She flashed a joking smile.

"No, ma'am!" He laughed. "Actually, you won't have time to do that. You'll be working. See, you're still the new girl here and that means, as the low woman on the totem pole, you'll spend most of your time with the rest of our surplus."

"Surplus?"

He waved her to follow him outside. On the other side of the back door was a short walkway leading to the back parking lot where employees parked or were dropped off. On the way to the lot was a large metal door, not unlike the one for the walk-in cooler inside the store.

Jason marched up to the door, yanked the metal handle, and pulled it open. A blast of cold air punched her in the face, and she raised her eyebrows at the stacks and stacks of boxes on the inside.

"This is our surplus." He slapped the top of the frozen box in front of them and pointed them out, one by one. "We have cod…walleye…shrimp…catfish…and lake perch. These are our most popular fish during Lent."

He stepped out of the cooler and slammed it shut, then grabbed a long stainless-steel table that was folded up against the wall next to the door leading into the store. "Give me a hand with this, will you?"

The two of them unfolded the table, flipped the legs out, and stood it securely. He dragged it along the pavement until it was situated behind a wooden fence that blocked the view from the small outside dining area. When he was satisfied with its position, he slapped the top of the table like he had the box in the cooler. This time, the slap was loud and echoed for a moment. "This is where you'll set up shop for the rest of the day."

"What do I do?"

"First, you grab disinfectant from the shelf on the inside of the back door. There's some on the second shelf. Use it and a roll of paper towels to scrub the top of this table. That way, if you drop any fish onto it, you can still use it. Otherwise, this thing is probably loaded with germs. When that's done, set up your bins and breading, and you'll bread all that fish in those boxes."

"All of them?" She had never breaded so much fish in one shift. Normally, she would bread a box or two on a really busy week.

Jason nodded. "Oh, yeah. I guarantee you, we will sell all this fish. We always do. It won't be the most interesting job in the world, but it has to be done."

She looked at the table, then nodded. "Okay, I'll get on it. What do you want me to do when I'm done?"

He released a belly laugh. "Let's take it one step at a time. I'll be shocked if you get it all done before the end of your shift. We'll see when we cross that bridge." He hitched his apron over the edge of his portly belly. "Take breaks when you need to but try to keep up. We'll start dipping into this stash tonight already, so we don't want to run out."

After he left her, she located the cleaner and a roll of paper towels, then sprayed the table down. While she was wiping it, her coworker Elena walked past her, arriving for her shift. She wore a self-satisfied smile on her face. "Ah, they got you doing all the breading this year?"

"It looks that way."

"Put some music on and let your mind wander. Otherwise, you'll go crazy. Actually, there's a spare radio inside. I'll grab it for you."

"Thanks." Vickie appreciated her coworker looking out for her. Some of them weren't particularly friendly, but Elena treated her well.

The woman returned with a small clock radio. "It's, like, a billion years old, but it'll work." She plugged it in and tuned it to a Top 40 station before she propped it on the fence. "There. It'll keep your mind busy. By the time you start breading the third box, you'll think you're going insane." She laughed and turned to head into the store for her shift.

One by one, her coworkers walked past and greeted her with laughter as they all commented on how happy they were to not have to do that job that evening.

Vickie set up a few bins for breading, along with a massive box of breadcrumbs. Once she felt she was ready to deliver, she removed the first huge box of cod from the walk-in freezer. She tore the box open to find layers of almost frozen fish.

She sighed quietly and set to work, tossing fish pieces into the bins and breading them. The music helped, but she was still alone, staring at a wooden fence. It was brutally boring.

I don't want to do this all night. She looked around for a second to make sure the coast was clear. Satisfied that she was completely alone and unobserved, she closed her eyes and took a few deep breaths. Her blood immediately began to rush again.

The vampire was about to unleash her super-speed when the back door flew open and Jason walked out. "How's it going out here?" He gave her a big smile.

"Oh…um, fine," she blurted. Now that the super-energy coursed through her veins, she was jittery and anxious to release it. Unfortunately, she couldn't do that while he stood there. "I'm…uh, getting going here."

He folded his hands behind his back. "It looks good. You have everything you need. I know we don't normally bread frozen fish, but in this case, we don't have much of a choice."

"Of course." She tapped her foot and tried to do whatever she could to keep the energy under control.

He pointed to the radio. "That's a good idea. Something to occupy yourself." He chuckled.

Vickie's eyes widened with her internal struggle. *Come on, leave me alone so I can do this.* "Yeah, that was Elena's idea."

"Smart." He took a deep breath. "Well, I'll let you get back to it. We're about to experience the first rush already, and I want all hands on deck in there. Keep at it." He sauntered away and into the store.

Once he was gone, she exhaled sharply, unleashed her super speed, and breaded the rest of the first box of cod in a few seconds. Hundreds of pieces of fish flipped and tossed with the breadcrumbs and landed safely in a bin for storage. She placed a lid on it and carried it back to the freezer, where she found another bin and repeated the process.

The first rush of the evening was the safest time to use her speed. As long as the store was busy, nobody would have time to come out and check on her.

She plowed her way through six boxes of cod and managed to bread and store all of them in under two minutes. When she was done, she placed her hands on the top of the table to steady herself. *Okay, you've earned a break.*

Vickie pulled her phone out and opened Facebook. She knew it was a mistake as that photo of her zit would still be there, but like most high school kids, it was her first instinct.

Sure enough, some of the kids in school had graduated to making memes out of the photo, including captions like:

WHEN SANTA WANTS YOU LOOKING YOUR BEST REINDEER GIRLS BE LIKE

And *BOZO THE CLOWN'S TRUE IDENTITY REVEALED!*

Vickie couldn't explain why the captions hurt her feelings. *These are stupid, lazy, and pointless. They don't hurt me. Why does this bother me so much?*

When she realized that staring at her phone would only make her more crabby, she opted to set up for the next round of breading. This time, she had three full boxes of walleye to deal with.

She completed the job in about forty-five seconds and earned herself another break. As she threw the last bin of breaded walleye into the cooler, Jason emerged from the store to check on her once again.

"Do you need anything? How's it going out here?"

"Just fine. I've finished the cod and the walleye."

His mouth dropped. "Already? That was fast." He walked into the cooler to make sure she had done it correctly. Sure enough, everything checked out. "All right...well, nice work. Keep it up. Take a break if you want. You've earned it. We're in a short lull at the moment. Do you want a sandwich?"

"Yes, I do!" The words were music to Vickie's ears. She was starving, and Al's had an open policy that allowed employees to eat when it wasn't busy.

She walked into the store and headed to the kitchen. A

few minutes later, she stood at the counter in the back storage room with a plate of fries and a fried cod sandwich, complete with a tall cup of Pepsi.

This isn't so bad. The work is easy enough and I'm eating like a champ. At least they feed you here.

A few coworkers made snide comments to her while they walked past, joking about the times they had to do all the breading for Lent. Vickie agreed with them and tried to sound like she understood what they were talking about.

But the job wasn't annoying for her. *As long as I have this super-speed, any of these boring tasks become a lot more manageable. It sure comes in handy when I need it.*

She scarfed the last bite of her sandwich, tossed the plate and cup into the dishwashing room, and returned to breading outside.

CHAPTER TEN

It was a cloudy Monday morning, and Vickie had just stepped out of the shower and prepared herself for the day. She walked into the kitchen to find Alexis shaking her head while she leaned against the counter. One of the lower cupboards stood open.

"Hey." She walked cautiously into the room. "What's wrong?"

The other girl folded her arms in front of her and spoke with a sharp tone. "I thought I would sit down this morning for breakfast with a box of cereal. But wouldn't you know it? They're all gone."

Vickie gritted her teeth and winced. "Oh."

"Yeah...oh." Alexis never looked this awake at this time of the morning, but her eyes were wide and full of fire. "There were three different boxes of cereal in this cupboard yesterday. What happened to them, I wonder?"

She was about to open her mouth and answer but she knew that her sister wasn't actually looking for an answer to the question. They both knew.

"Then I figured I would eat a bagel with cream cheese. I was in the mood for cereal, but a bagel would be fine. It would fill me up." Alexis shrugged. "Did I find any bagels in the fridge?"

The vampire shook her head silently.

"Of course not. All you're doing is eating everything without thinking about who else is in this house. Maybe my dad can cook himself eggs and bacon for breakfast, but you and I don't have that much time, do we? We have ten minutes to eat something before our ride is here, and I don't know what I'm going to eat."

"I was hungry last night." Vickie wasn't sure what the big deal was. "I had a long shift at work and I needed to eat. That's all that was around."

"And you didn't think about the fact that emptying the cupboards might be a bad thing for the rest of us?"

Now, she was getting annoyed. She didn't like being talked down to. "Look, I get that you're hungry, but all I did was eat some food. It's fine. We'll get more. Why do you have to have such an attitude about it?"

Alexis rolled her eyes and walked past her. "You don't get it."

"Tell me what I'm supposed to get."

She raised her palms in confusion as Alexis spun to face her. "Everything in this house has been about you since you got here. I was happy to help you, but you don't care how any of this affects anyone other than you. You eat all the food in the house for some reason, but we have to sit around and be hungry. It's exactly like it was with Will."

"What does any of this have to do with Will? I thought we were talking about food."

"It's all the same, Vickie. You look at everything through your eyes and not through anyone else's. You knew Will was a Sang, but you didn't say anything because you didn't want me to be mad at you. Never mind that it put my life in danger. It's the same thing here. You look at the food in terms of how it affects you and not everyone else."

Vickie put her hands on her hips. "Well excuse me for having a hard time. You know I've been here a little more than half a year, and I wasn't even in this century earlier. I'm still trying to figure things out. I don't know how to be a vampire in this world. It's harder than you think."

Alexis wore a deflated look. "And see? How quickly this conversation becomes about you and how things are hard for you. You might be a vampire, but the rest of us have to live with a vampire. And it's hard for us, too." She marched down the hall and to her room where she packed her backpack.

She was starving, but she was so distracted and upset about the argument that she didn't bother to even try to find something to eat. The two of them climbed into the car in silence and with cold looks on their faces, and they rode to school without a word. Both of them were incredibly hungry.

After they got out of the car, she hung back for a moment to let her sister walk ahead of her. She walked out the parking lot to go across the street and grab breakfast from Bruegger's Bagels. Vickie turned right at the top of the parking lot to go into the supermarket instead.

She bought a breakfast sandwich, returned to the school, and went to the cafeteria where she could heat it and eat it before the day started. The sandwich was dry and tasteless and it wasn't very satisfying. But it beat walking with Alexis to the bagel shop in awkward, angry silence.

As she chewed on the rubbery sandwich, Vickie shook her head and looked out the cafeteria window. *Is this what it's like to have siblings in today's world? I don't remember being this upset and irritated at my brother and sister back home. We never fought like this. Is it because she's human and I'm a vampire? Are we simply too different to live together? Am I doing something wrong?*

In the middle of the day, she walked into the library during her study period and found a seat at the table across from Tricia.

"What's wrong?" the girl asked as the bell rang announcing the start of the period.

"Nothing." She wasn't in the mood to talk about it and she didn't think anyone could help anyway.

Tricia tilted her head with skepticism. "Give me a break. You're wearing it all over your face. You're terrible at hiding your emotions. What's wrong?"

She sighed. "I'm fighting with Alexis, that's all."

"Ahhhh…" She gave her a knowing nod. "You know, when two girls live together, they fight. It's the law, I think." She giggled. "What's the fight about?"

"She's mad at me because I ate a big meal last night. I used most of the food that was lying around, and she didn't have time to make breakfast this morning."

"That's it?"

"Yep." She conveniently—and deliberately—left out the

"I knew her boyfriend was a blood-sucking monster but chose not to tell her" part of the argument.

"Well, that's stupid." Tricia twisted her face into a grimace. "Food is nothing to fight over. Besides, if you were that hungry, you needed to eat, right?"

"I was starving."

"Okay, well, there you go. Sometimes, you need to eat a lot. That's okay. Shoot, I come from a house where you're on your own for meals every day. If you don't eat and someone else eats the food you wanted, that's on you. You should've gotten up and eaten it first. We all subscribe to the first-come, first-served idea."

"I like that." Vickie nodded. It made so much sense to her. She knew it would never happen in the house she was living in, but she thought the idea would work.

"Is that all you're fighting about?"

"Eh, it's all kinds of stuff." Vickie pulled a textbook from her backpack. "Lately, we fight often. I don't know why."

"It's because you live together," Tricia said matter-of-factly. "Sometimes, you fight. And those fights can take a few days before they blow over."

"This has been going on for days now." She frowned as she thought about that. "I hate it. I don't like fighting with her. But for whatever reason, she's been really angry and resentful toward me. I'm not trying to do anything to hurt her or make her mad. I'm only trying to be me."

"Of course you are." The girl popped a bubble in her mouth from the gum she was chewing. "Just because you fight doesn't mean you're a bad person. She's probably in the wrong and doesn't even know it yet."

Another statement that made sense to Vickie. "What should I do?"

Tricia leaned back in her chair and folded her hands behind her head. "The way I see it, you need a break from her. Get yourself a little space between the two of you until things can calm down."

"I do need that. We all eat at the dinner table, and that's the only time I really see or talk to her at home."

Her companion seemed taken aback by the statement. "You eat at the dinner table? As a family?"

"Yeah."

"Wow. I didn't think anybody did that anymore. My family eats off TV trays in the living room at dinnertime." She burst out laughing. Vickie joined in, although she wasn't quite sure what was funny about it.

"How do I get space then?" She didn't have a car or other friends to hang out with besides Eric.

"What are you doing Friday night?"

She thought for a moment. "Nothing. Eric is out of town, so I will be sitting at home and watching TV like I always am."

Tricia leaned forward. "Perfect. You can come over to my house."

"Why?"

"I want to show you a good time. We'll hang out and chill for a while. You need to be able to get away from it all. No fighting, no bickering…just hang out. We'll watch a movie or something. Keep it really laid back."

"That sounds good. I think I would like that." Vickie gave her a warm smile, which she returned.

As they dove into their homework, her stomach fluttered with excitement. *Now you're really making friends. You won't have to hang out at Johnny V's with Alexis all the time, and you can have a place to go when you have these problems with Alexis. It's perfect. You'll have so much fun.*

They continued to work throughout the period, but every once in a while, she looked away from her books at Tricia. *She's funny, friendly, and she takes care of the people she likes. I talk to her about my problems and she is right there to help me. Maybe Tricia is the sister I never had. We'll have fun this weekend.*

The bell rang and they tucked their textbooks into their backpacks. "Another day flying by," Tricia moaned.

"Well, now I'm all excited about the weekend." Vickie gave her a huge smile.

"Me too. It'll be fun. Remember, no fighting, no awkwardness…just friends hanging out, having a good time, and forgetting about everything that's bothering them. Like homework. Or sisters." She winked at Vickie, who laughed at the statement.

My own friend. Not a friend of Alexis' who also hangs out with me. My own, personal, good friend. She likes me for me, not because I am with Alexis all the time. This will be great.

CHAPTER ELEVEN

Craig zipped his overnight bag and squeezed the sides so he could bring the teeth of the zipper together without breaking it.

He stood and sighed, then nodded. *Who says I need a suitcase for four days' of clothes?*

That had been another one of Carol's pet peeves. Whenever they went on vacation together, he could cram a week's worth of clothes into a duffel bag, while she packed two or three suitcases.

She could never understand how he packed so light. With a glint in his eye, he looked up and winked at his departed wife. *I've still got it, babe.*

Despite his ability to pack efficiently, the bag still weighed a considerable amount, so he grunted as he threw the strap over his shoulder and picked it up off his bed. He then picked up his laptop in its protective sleeve and walked out the bedroom door and down into the kitchen.

"Okay, girls!" he shouted. The two bedroom doors opened and the girls stumbled out, both groggy.

Alexis rubbed her face. "Dad, do you really have to leave this early?" she asked with a yawn. "The sun isn't even up yet."

"I know, hon, but Chicago traffic is brutal." He dropped the bag and the laptop onto the kitchen table. "The earlier I can leave, the better. I'll grab a coffee on my way out, don't worry." He stood in front of them, wide-eyed and ready for the excitement of the day. He stood in stark contrast to the listless, eyes-half-opened lack of energy that came from the girls.

"Have fun," Vickie mumbled, still trying to muster some wakefulness.

He looked from one to the other while he ran through his mental check list. After Monday's breakfast debacle—which Alexis had complained about loudly and vociferously—he'd squeezed in a trip to the store. If nothing else, the cupboards were now fully stocked. Unfortunately, that did little to ease the obvious tension that still defined his daughters.

"Girls, I'll come back on Sunday. That leaves you four days of freedom. Know that this is a big responsibility and I am placing my trust in you both." They nodded. "Please get along, relax, and enjoy a little freedom, but don't have too much fun."

Neither girl looked at the other.

Craig shook his head. *They've really become siblings, all right. Oh, to think of the grudges I held against my brothers.* "And look, I know you two aren't exactly buddies at the moment but don't fight or any of that nonsense. This is a chance for you two to have fun and enjoy the whole house. Don't spoil it. Please. For me."

Alexis sent Vickie a sidelong glance, then pursed her lips and nodded. "Fine, Dad."

"The cupboards are full, so you shouldn't need to go anywhere. But if you do run out of something, I've left a few bucks on the counter. Don't spend it unless you need to. And keep the receipts."

She laughed. "You don't trust us?"

"Not with my money, I don't." He smiled at her. "I expect you both to keep the place clean. Don't throw any parties or have any friends over. I mean that. Keep it a quiet weekend for yourselves."

They agreed and he stepped forward and wrapped his arms around his daughter. "Are you sure you'll be okay? I can stay, you know."

"Dad, give it a rest. We'll be fine. Really. You need to do this. I won't pick any fights this weekend." He kissed her on the forehead.

He stepped to Vickie and gave her a big hug as well. "Only to school and back, okay? Try to make some of the food last."

She giggled. "I will."

Craig took a deep breath and shouldered his bag, then pressed the button on the garage door remote. "Girls, I'll text you when I get to the hotel. It should be in about two hours, maybe two and a half, so you'll get that text by lunchtime. If you need anything, let me know and I can come home."

"All right, all right, Dad. You'll be late." Alexis walked up and gave him a playful shove on his shoulder. "We'll be fine. We know what to do. Hit the road, or you'll waste this early wake-up time."

He nodded, looked at the door, then back at the girls. "Love you both."

"We love you too." Vickie smiled.

He walked out the door and pulled it shut behind him. It echoed in the otherwise silent house.

The vampire looked at the clock, which read 5:12 a.m. "Will you take a shower or go back to bed?"

Alexis shook her head. "I have half an hour until I need to be up. I'm going to bed." Both girls returned to their rooms and tried to fall asleep again.

Outside, Craig tossed his bags into the back of the SUV, climbed in, and set his GPS for the Chicago Hilton. As he backed out of the driveway, he stared at the darkened house. *They must have gone back to bed. Please be okay while I'm gone, girls. Please.*

While he drove down the road, he swallowed a lump in his throat. He was looking forward to this trip, but this was the first time he would leave the girls for an extended period of time. Even worse, this was the first time he was leaving Alexis since her mother died.

His mind raced with possibilities. *What if the house burns down? What if Vickie loses control of her powers and does something horrible? What if the Circle comes back or something? What if they get into an accident or get lost and they can't get help?*

Consciously, he knew this was merely his brain making him paranoid. The girls were both responsible, and he knew they would be fine. Still, the emotion of leaving them made everything go haywire.

He pulled through a drive-thru for a cup of coffee and placed it in the cup holder to cool. Rather than blast music, he pulled up an old Jerry Seinfeld stand-up comedy album to keep himself awake and alert as he drove.

"I was the best man to a wedding one time, that was pretty good. Pretty good title, I thought, "best man." I thought it was a bit much. I thought we'd have the groom and a pretty good man. That's more than enough. If I'm the best man, why is she marrying him?"

Craig laughed. He'd heard that joke so many times but it always cracked him up. Having comedy on in the car was a relief for him. Sharing the car with the girls meant letting them choose the radio station. They were never in the mood to listen to comedy.

He rolled the window down for a little fresh air and smiled. *Freedom. That's what this is. It may only be for a few days, but it's freedom. I am free to be myself for a while. This isn't too bad.* He sipped his caramel macchiato while he pulled onto the freeway.

A couple of hours later, Craig sat gridlocked in downtown Chicago. Horns honked and everyone moved at a rate of a few inches a minute. He rested his head on the headrest behind him and stared down his nose out the windshield at the large billboards. *Why do they still make billboards? Does anyone buy anything because they saw it on a billboard?*

The SUV crept along slowly. He glanced at the GPS. *I'm only a few miles away from the hotel, but it'll take me over half an hour to get there from here. I could get out and walk and be there faster.*

Carol had always wanted to move to a big city like Chicago, but he never did. This type of traffic was one of the biggest reasons why.

Meanwhile, he kept his temper at bay with his comedy albums, which had now moved on to Jim Gaffigan.

"You know what it's like having five kids? Imagine you're drowning...and someone hands you a baby."

Craig laughed again. If it wasn't for the constant stream of jokes from his car speakers, he would be squeezing the steering wheel with road rage.

Eventually, he reached the towering Chicago Hilton. He pulled up in front of the main entrance and retrieved his bag. The valet took his SUV to park it, and he walked up the steps.

Already, the hotel bustled with activity. Podcasters from all over the country had descended on the establishment. For a moment, he couldn't appreciate the opulent, cavernous lobby of the hotel because he was surprised at how many people were attending.

But once he got in line at the front desk, he stared at his surroundings. Carpeted staircases spiraled in all directions. A large grandfather clock stood in the center of the hall.

Booths lined the walls, and he shook his head at how big everything felt.

After checking in, he took a few steps to the side to survey the situation. *Sometimes, you feel like you live in a big city and then you go to an actual big city. This is crazy. There is nothing like this in Milwaukee at all.*

As he stepped onto the elevator, he thought about the last time he had been in Chicago.

He had taken Carol to a special oncologist for treatment. She had spent a couple of weeks being treated, although it didn't do much for her cancer. He smiled as he thought about sitting in the hospital courtyard with her.

At the time, they sat at a picnic table. Cords and IVs came out of the ports in her body beneath her gown. She still looked happy and radiant. Carol held his hand and laughed about how she loved taking romantic trips into the city with him.

She always kept the mood light, even in the darkest times.

He stepped off the elevator onto the fifth floor. While he wandered down the hall, looking for his room, he daydreamed to a time even further back when he was in Chicago for a journalism conference years prior.

This was before Alexis was born. And while he'd enjoyed himself, he didn't feel it did much to further his career. When the opportunity came along in the years following, he always declined.

A couple of younger men in their mid-twenties greeted him as he walked past them. One of them held his phone out and was recording the other one. He didn't think much of it until he opened his hotel room door and closed it behind him.

Those guys are recording a podcast, or live-streaming, or something. I didn't bring any of my podcasting stuff. Should I have? Is this my inexperience at play? Maybe this was a mistake. I've only been podcasting for a little while—successfully, anyway. Once I go down there, I'll be exposed as an inexperienced fake. I know it. They're all prepared for this. I'm not. I'll walk around and take notes on my phone like a goofus. They'll sniff me out right away.

As the stream of doubts filtered through his brain, Craig suddenly felt Carol put her hand on his shoulder and whisper, *Craig, shut up and get over yourself. You're fine.*

Go down there and be yourself. Learn from it, don't hide from it.

With a deep breath, he dropped his bags on the bed, pulled out the registration packet he'd received in the mail, and slipped the lanyard attached to the tag that read *CRAIG WATSON - The Truth About...* around his neck.

He looked in the mirror. "You're a professional podcaster like them. Go down there and mingle. This cost you money. Don't spend all that to play small."

With a forced confidence in his step, he walked out of the hotel room and headed down to the lobby to start networking with the other attendees.

CHAPTER TWELVE

Neither girl fell asleep again that morning. The interruption kept their mind racing. Both were excited to have a weekend of freedom, even though they weren't getting along at the time.

For Vickie, it was merely the chance to hang out at home and relax a little bit. And for Alexis, it was the chance to enjoy some independence—something every teenager craved.

As the vampire ate breakfast after her shower, she was struck by how quiet the house was. Usually, by this time in the morning, Craig was up and talking to them both. Or maybe he would have the TV on in the living room. Either way, there was always noise.

But that morning, she looked up from her cereal bowl to see her sister staring at her phone while she took another spoonful of hers. The silence was almost more annoying than the usual noise.

Once they reached school, they separated for the day. When Alexis made it to her locker, Jess was waiting for her.

"Good morning!" she greeted her with a smile. "So, Independent Woman, your dad left this morning, hey?"

She pulled her locker open and unzipped her backpack. "Yep. He's gone for four days."

"What time is the party?" Her friend winked at her.

"Ha-ha, very funny. Like I could even throw a party. Besides, Vickie would probably wind up being the life of the party anyway. Or she'd burn the house down showing off something stupid to my friends." She dropped a few books in her locker and grabbed a notebook off the top shelf.

Jess tilted her head. "Is everything all right with you two? It sounds like there's some tension."

"Tension?" She scoffed. "I'm simply getting tired of her. I know she's from a different country and everything, but every decision she makes is about her. She only thinks about how things affect her and nobody else. It's annoying to live with."

"She doesn't seem like the type." The other girl shook her head. "Maybe a little naive at times, but not selfish."

Alexis turned to look at her. "Trust me. And even if it's not intentional, it's still a big deal, right? It's annoying to live with someone like that. I have a life to live, too, you know."

Jess grabbed the straps of her backpack and pulled them together. "She probably only needs a little guidance. That's why she's here. She's looking for somebody to help her navigate life. That's you."

She knew her friend was right and that she needed to keep Vickie's inexperience with the world in mind but it still bothered her. "I don't want to be, like, a jerk to her. I know she's trying. But I am still trying to figure out my life too, and every time I turn around, Vickie needs babysitting again. It gets old."

Jess put her hand on her shoulder. She knew Alexis was talking about missing her mom. "This will all work itself out. I know it will. You both are good people and are only going through a little rough patch."

"I don't want to think about it anymore. I'll be around her all weekend. I can deal with it then."

Later that day, Vickie had to admit she hadn't planned her weekend properly.

"I completely forgot that Alexis and I will be home alone this weekend." She shrugged at Tricia. "I can't get together on Friday. I don't have a ride."

"Dang." Tricia was looking forward to the company. She didn't have friends over very often. "We'll have to plan it for, like, next week or something. So you're simply going to sit around all weekend with Alexis?"

"Ugh. Yeah, that's pretty much all I'll do."

The other girl leaned in. "That sounded like you aren't looking forward to it. You and Alexis don't get along?"

"We do. Not lately, though. So no, I guess not. The problem is, I don't even really know why. I try my best but I keep screwing up. I try to be a good sister to her and she gets mad at me."

Tricia pushed her homework aside. She was much more interested in the conversation. "What are you doing about it?"

"What do you mean?"

"Like, do you yell back? Do you fight? Or do you refuse to do what she says?"

"I...I don't know."

"That means you don't. Look, if she pushes you around, you have to push back. Remember when Megan Fitz gave you all that grief so you took the fight right to her in the cafeteria?"

Vickie winced at the thought. "I got detention for that."

"Right, but you won't get detention for fighting back at home."

Her mind raced at what Tricia implied. She thought of when she accidentally injured Alexis when she threw her over the bed a few months before. The feeling of hurting her was so painful, she swore she wouldn't do it again.

The other girl shrugged and pulled her homework closer. "Suit yourself. I'm simply saying, the fastest way to get someone to respect you is by not doing every little thing they want you to do. You have to stand up for yourself."

Vickie nodded. "Where did you learn this?"

"Life, babe. I have enough stuff I have to fight against, too. Life will swallow you whole if you roll over every time someone wants you to do something."

"How do I do that?" She folded her hands on the table. "How do I fight back? I don't want to hurt Alexis."

"No, no, no, that's not what I mean. I only mean you have to stand up for yourself. That's all. If she treats you like someone who can't make decisions for herself or someone who needs to be bossed around, throw that right back in her face. You don't have to be mean about it but be firm. Make it clear that you are your own person and you can choose to do something or not do something. If she wants something out of life, she can get it herself. You don't owe her anything."

The girls began to do their homework, but Vickie's mind continued to race. *I don't owe her anything? I'm not sure about that part. She and her dad helped bring me to America and gave me a second lease on life. They've protected me and helped me. I kinda owe her something, don't I?*

At the end of the day, the girls rode silently back to the house. They walked in and Alexis immediately approached the chores list that rested on the counter. "Today, we have to dust and vacuum. This weekend, we'll wash all the windows and the floors." She tossed the sheet of paper onto the counter. "You know, if you did all that tonight, we could spend the rest of the weekend doing whatever we wanted."

Vickie tossed her backpack onto the kitchen table. "Don't you mean, if we do all of that tonight?"

"Why would we? You have all the power. You could get this done in seconds."

"That doesn't matter." Vickie raised the tone of her voice, which caught Alexis off-guard. "I'm not here to do your bidding. Maybe you can do all the cleaning."

"Vickie, think about it. You can clean the entire house in less than a few minutes. If I joined in, I would simply slow the operation down to a crawl."

"I do all the work while you sit around." She shook her head. "Unbelievable."

"Would you rather we both clean for hours while we complain to each other, or would you rather tap into that super-speed of yours and knock this whole thing out? Then we can spend the rest of the weekend relaxing and doing whatever we want. That's the one thing Dad doesn't let you do, right?"

She was right. Craig focused on making sure the vampire could do things at normal speed so that she would understand the responsibilities that she was taking on. His goal was always to make sure she developed like a normal teenage girl, rather than a super-powered vampire.

"That part is great, but I'll still do all the work then. Even I know that isn't fair. You get to sit around and be lazy."

Alexis was stuck for a second. She couldn't argue the point, but she also really wanted to avoid the cleaning. "I'll tell you what—if you do the cleaning, I'll order pizza tonight." Vickie had developed a love for pizza. "We'll get two pizzas, one with whatever you want on it. And that cash on the counter can be yours."

The cash had been left by Craig for emergencies. In Alexis's mind, this was important enough to use it.

"What's the catch?" Vickie had a feeling there was something else and that the other girl was manipulating her. Tricia had really gotten through.

"No catch. Do the job and you'll get the money and the pizza. We can leave each other alone for the whole rest of the weekend."

She stared at the money on the counter and she thought about how right Alexis really was. "Fine. I'll do it."

"Awesome. I'll be in my room. I'll order the pizza and it'll come after you get done cleaning." She disappeared down the hall and closed her bedroom door behind her.

Sighing, the vampire walked to the sink and opened the cupboard under it to find a dust rag. She looked around the kitchen. *Alexis is totally taking advantage of you. But shoot, you get extra money out of it, plus an entire weekend to hang out and do nothing, I guess. There's not much else I can do, except...*

With a deep breath, Vickie closed her eyes and activated her super-speed. Gripping the dust rag tightly, she sprinted from room to room and cleaned every corner and every nook and cranny that collected dust.

Meanwhile, Alexis had put headphones on and sat on her phone in her room.

Once the dusting was done, Vickie pulled the vacuum cleaner out of the front closet. "Okay, time to really get down to it." She turned the cleaner on and rushed through the house, trying to get the job done in time for her pizza reward.

While she heard the vacuum cleaner, Alexis smiled to herself. *It was like shooting fish in a barrel. This is perfect. I don't know why Dad resists this stuff.*

As she neared the end of her vacuuming routine, Vickie's stomach rumbled. She hoped the pizza would arrive soon since she was suddenly starving. *All this running around really screws with my system. I can't wait to sink my teeth into that pizza.*

CHAPTER THIRTEEN

"They plan to do something."

Those were the words that came out of Krista's mouth as she and Vickie walked through the halls on the way to gym class.

"What do you mean, something?" Vickie had a feeling that this zit issue wouldn't go away quietly. Still, she wasn't sure how these things were handled in the twenty-first-century high school atmosphere.

"I don't know." Her friend sighed. "It's so stupid. But I caught wind that a group of people was planning something for gym today. I never heard what. They had a private Facebook Group going, I guess. It's probably really stupid. I wouldn't worry too much about it."

On the surface, she wasn't worried. How badly could they really embarrass her? But at the same time, would this be one of those annoyances that never went away?

Krista opened the locker room door for her, and the two of them walked in. At first, it didn't appear as though anything was different. All the girls in the locker room were changing into their gym clothes, some quietly, while others joked around with each other.

She shrugged and leaned over to whisper, "Maybe I heard it wrong. Everyone seems fine here."

Vickie nodded in response, but she knew that it wasn't what it seemed. Her senses worked overtime trying to decipher the mood of the room. Some girls gave off a sense of guilt. Others appeared mischievous. And while the group overall did an excellent job of hiding it on the outside, she could sense the inside. She knew they were planning something, and it felt like it was most of the class.

As she opened her locker and pulled out her t-shirt with the Clear Lake High School Gym Department logo emblazoned across the front, Abby Fontaine sat on a bench next to her, tying her shoes.

"Hi, Vickie." Her voice dripped with insincerity. "How are you today?"

She turned to see the fake smile. "Fine, Abby."

"Oh, that's good. I hear we're doing volleyball today. Isn't that fun?"

The vampire didn't buy it. It was as though the girl tried to lull her into a false sense of security so that the eventual drop would be even more dramatic and more entertaining for her. She refused to respond to any more comments from her.

"The silent treatment, hey? Well, I suppose I understand. I posted that photo of you on Facebook, and that was really mean of me. I thought it was funny at the time, but it was embarrassing for you. I'm sorry."

Other girls might have fallen for the ruse, but not

Vickie. *There's not an ounce of that apology that is sincere. Who does she think she's trying to fool?*

Vickie and Krista walked out to the gym, where three volleyball nets cut the area in half lengthwise. None of the other girls were out of the locker room yet.

"This is weird." Krista looked around. A few boys milled about but no girls had appeared. "Why haven't any of them come out yet?"

The vampire rolled her eyes. "They will." Her senses told her that this would be the something.

All at once, the girls poured out of the locker room and each of them wore a bright red foam clown nose on her face. Some of them played along quietly. Others were obnoxious, doing cartwheels and cheering.

They circled Vickie and honked their noses at her as they squeezed them. She tried not to show that she was bothered by this silly routine. *This is a waste of time. So why does this bother me as much as it does?*

When Mr. Kolander, the gym teacher, approached, he asked them to take the noses off. "I don't know what this is about, but you can't play any games with clown noses on."

"Sorry, Mr. Kolander, we're only trying to fit in with some of the other, more prominent red noses in our class." Abby knew how to be annoying, that was for sure.

Krista gave her friend a concerned look. "Are you okay?"

"Yeah. That was stupid." Vickie shook her head. Still, her mind raced as she thought of them all circling around her, laughing at her for having a zit. All she wanted to do was fire up her speed and strength and plow through all of them, laying waste to the whole class and leaving bodies piled up while she walked away.

But she knew better. And at least she had Krista on her side.

Mr. Kolander tucked a volleyball under his arm and began to explain the rules of the sport. Once in a while, Vickie's gaze would drift to Abby, who wore a satisfied grin on her face for being able to pull the stunt off.

They paired off into teams that rotated from net to net while everyone not on the court had to volley back and forth to practice. Krista and Vickie were the first team, and on the opposite end of the court were Abby and Shelly.

After the first session was over, the two teams moved within one court of each other. That's when Abby began to see her opportunities.

Vickie lined up to serve the volleyball. As she tossed it into the air, another volleyball rocketed past her and narrowly missed her nose. The close call knocked her off-balance, and she fell awkwardly. She sat and looked around, confused. "Who did that? What happened?"

"It was only a wild shot, Vickie, don't worry about it." Mr. Kolander didn't seem too concerned with it. "It didn't hit you, did it?"

Krista helped her to her feet. "No. It didn't hit me. It came close, though."

"Keep your heads on a swivel, everyone," Mr. Kolander shouted. "Errant shots happen all the time when you play this closely together. Do your best to keep the ball under control."

As they continued to play, Vickie noticed some of the girls smirking at her. *I don't even have a zit on my nose anymore. What is the big deal?* She shrugged it aside and focused on playing volleyball.

A few minutes later, another ball careened past her and this time, bounced off her shoulder. "Hey!" She spun and a few of the girls at the next court laughed.

"Sorry, Vickie!" one of them shouted in response. Abby laughed and shook her head in the background.

Vickie and Krista huddled together for a moment. "Why does it feel like all these girls are targeting me?"

Krista shook her head. "I don't know. I think they're picking on you. Don't let them see that it's bothering you or they'll keep it up. Seriously, forget about it and keep playing."

Mr. Kolander blew his whistle to indicate that the teams needed to switch courts again. Now, Krista and Vickie were lined up across from Abby and Shelly. A devilish grin spread across Abby's face as she tucked a strand of dark hair behind her ear and tightened her ponytail.

"Okay, these girls are good." Krista clapped sharply. "Abby plays on the varsity volleyball team. Shelly plays soccer, so she's an athlete too. They're fast and Abby's tall. Stay on your toes."

The two teams began the game and each team scored a few points. Vickie desperately wanted to tap into her powers and put Abby in her place, but she continued to limit herself to keep the game close and believable.

As her adversary stood behind the line to serve, she looked at Sarah, a girl on one of the other teams. She cocked her eyebrow and nodded once, then tossed the ball in the air.

"Hey, Vickie!" Sarah called and Vickie turned to look at her.

Abby took advantage of the distraction and delivered a perfect serve in the vampire's direction. Before she could react, the ball caught her squarely in the face, bounced off her nose, and launched her to land on her back, flat as a pancake on the gym floor.

Mr. Kolander blew the whistle again to stop the action. Krista ran over to check on her. "Are you okay?"

She blinked a few times as tears filled her eyes. She wasn't hurt so badly that she was crying, but the blow to the face had caused her eyes to water involuntarily. Through her blurred vision, she recognized the outline of a tall, pony-tailed girl bent over with her hands on her knees.

"Oh, Vickie, are you okay?" That same insincere voice seemed to mock her with its false solicitude. "I'm so sorry. I was trying to serve and I guess it got away from me. I think this is why Mr. Kolander told us to pay attention to our game and not get distracted."

Vickie gritted her teeth. *Don't attack. Don't attack. Don't attack. Let her talk.*

Mr. Kolander kneeled beside Vickie, lifted her into a seated position, and put his thumbs on either side of her nose. "Yeah, that might be broken. I'll write you a pass to go to the school nurse and see if there's anything she can do. Otherwise, you'll have to go to the doctor."

As she rose to her feet, a trickle of blood dripped out of one of her nostrils. Krista ran and found her a towel to keep it at bay.

Her eyes stopped watering and she could see everyone

in the class staring at her. As Mr. Kolander's back was turned, Abby had put the foam red nose back on her face with a giant smile. "I guess we're back to being Bozo again, at least for a little while!" She laughed, and a few other girls stifled their laughter as well.

"Abby, don't be such a jerk." Krista scowled at her. "Vickie could be seriously hurt here."

The girl shrugged. "Oh, give me a break. She doesn't care if other people get hurt. You saw what she did to Megan."

"And Megan's fine." Krista put her arm around Vickie's shoulders.

"Whatever." Abby shook her head and pulled the nose off. "It's merely a little taste of her own medicine. That red will be much harder to hide than that zit you had, Vickie!"

She laughed while the two friends walked out of the gym and into the locker room, where the vampire was able to look at her nose in the mirror.

It was now swollen and a dark-burgundy color. "Wow. I really do look like a clown now."

"Don't worry about that." Krista waved it off. "Let me walk you to the nurse's office."

"No, that's fine. I can do it. Go back in there and I'll catch you later." She knew exactly what to do about this.

Krista agreed and left, leaving her alone in the locker room. Staring into the mirror, she took a deep breath and forced more energy through her body. In seconds, the swelling in her nose subsided, it shrank back to normal, and the redness faded. With a loud click, her nose popped into place, fully healed.

You have a pass to the nurse's office and everyone who saw your nose broken will be back here soon. Change your clothes and get out of here before they see you.

She changed and jogged into the hall. As the door closed, she could hear the laughter of the other girls in class leaving the gym.

Abby did that on purpose. She targeted me to embarrass me. How am I supposed to make this kind of thing stop? Can I, or will I have to deal with this for the rest of my high school life?

Frustrated, she walked down the hall, headed to her next class, and hoped nobody would notice that she never visited the school nurse.

CHAPTER FOURTEEN

The first day in Chicago had been a whirlwind for Craig.

He was always impressed by the city itself and walking around there made him feel like a big shot. But even more impressive was the atmosphere inside the hotel during the conference.

As he pulled up a stool at the hotel bar, sitting shoulder-to-shoulder with a crowd of podcasters of various ages, sizes, and backgrounds, he ordered a Miller Lite and took a deep breath.

He hadn't been prepared to be so overwhelmed. He estimated that he was accidentally in the background of at least twenty-five different YouTube shows. Some people had brought bags loaded with professional audio and video recording equipment.

"I had no idea there were so many different ways to record a conversation," he commented to a twenty-some-thing man who stood at one of the booths.

The man with thick black-framed glasses and a neck-beard that was several days old laughed with him. "How do you record your podcasts, sir?"

Ugh. He called me "sir." Way to make me feel like I'm a hundred years old, guy. "I simply have a Blue Yeti hooked up to my laptop."

The man twisted his face in disgust. "Seriously? That's it?"

Craig didn't understand the confusion. "What's the problem with that? All the blog posts I read said that the Blue Yeti was one of the top-of-the-line podcast microphones."

"Yeah, if you're starting out. But if you're here, man, you are obviously doing well enough to upgrade your equipment. For one thing, you really should look at something like the Shure SM7B Cardioid Dynamic Microphone. That's a pro's microphone, and it will blow whatever you record with the Yeti clear out of the water."

"I guess so." He didn't think there was any problem with his podcast sound. "I'll think about it."

"And then...you gotta go video, man." The man shook his head as if it was basic information that he should have known by then. "Everybody—all the best content creators —spend money on 4K camera equipment and they document their journeys using video platforms."

Document their journey? The language of this place is so awkward. "I've thought about it, but video gets complicated really quickly. I'm trying to do one thing really well right now, so I'm focused on audio. We're a lean team."

He picked up the lean team terminology from another podcaster he'd spoken to. Craig was proud that he could weave that into a conversation, even though his team was only himself.

"See, that's where the HitchPod comes in handy!" The man stretched his arms out as if to present his booth to Craig, who had already stood there for several minutes. He picked up a display model of a kind of tripod with a camera attached to it. "The HitchPod is the ultimate in flexible, hands-free video technology. You can hold it by hand like this, extend the legs and use it as a traditional tripod, or you can do this."

He squeezed the legs of the tripod together and flipped a plastic latch on the bottom of one of the legs, revealing a small clip. He attached the clip to the front of his belt and pulled a strap out of one of the other legs to secure the entire camera to his waist.

Craig stroked his chin and feigned interest in the product. "You attach the tripod to your belt?"

"Check it out, man." He held his hands in the air. "No hands. And I can move wherever I want to without losing my camera."

He was surprised to see how solid the HitchPod appeared to be as the camera hardly moved while the man waddled around the booth area.

Back at the bar that night, he withdrew the HitchPod business card out of his pocket and looked at it while he sipped his beer. *When did they start only putting websites on business cards, anyway? It's so weird. No phone number, no address, not even the guy's name. Who would I ask for? These kids today...*

Immediately, he felt regret at thinking that way. *These kids today are the reason why you have a business at all. Come on, man, you're not in your eighties, you're in your forties. There are many older guys here. You're here to learn. Don't give up on everything because it makes you uncomfortable.*

One thing he was bad at was making friends in unknown environments. Even though he promised himself he wouldn't spend every night holed up in his hotel, even glancing around the room made him feel nervous.

Who are you kidding? None of these people want to talk to you. Besides, they're all in groups already. You'd be infringing on a good time, I'm sure. And you'd make it awkward for everybody.

As he scanned the room, a redhead with curly hair and a pleasant smile made eye contact with him. He smiled politely and returned his attention to the TV behind the bar.

About ten minutes later, the group to his left exited the bar. The redhead walked up to the stools and took the one immediately next to him. "Finally!" She smiled and exhaled. "I've been standing for almost half an hour. I wanted to take a load off."

Craig nodded to her, and she ordered a beer. While she waited for it, she turned to him and extended her hand. "I'm Chelsea."

"Craig. Nice to meet you." He shook her hand, which she held onto for a half-second longer than him. "Are you a podcaster?"

"Oh yeah, like everyone else here." She giggled. "I host a show called *Refresh Your Food*. It's about how to cook healthy meals and refresh your life with the right ingredients."

He nodded. "It sounds interesting."

She gave him a toothy smile with warm and friendly

eyes squinting behind strong cheek muscles—the result of many smiles. "I love it. It's really become a passion of mine. What about you?"

"Oh, um..." He paused to think of how everyone had presented themselves to him. "I'm the host of a show called *The Truth About...* which focuses on digging deeper into topics of interest from a journalistic but human point of view."

"See, now that sounds interesting!" She laughed and thanked the bartender who poured her a beer. "What kinds of topics?"

"I've done health and disease-related stuff, but everything really took off this season when I started talking about blended families and non-traditional family units."

She leaned forward slightly, turned her body, and showed a deep interest in what he was saying. "Really? That sounds like a topic that many people would go for. What made you choose that?"

"Oh...um, it's not something I talk about much, but my family and I have gone through a host of changes in the past year." He stumbled through his explanation as he didn't really talk about it much outside of the podcast. "My wife passed away last year, and—"

"I am so sorry!" She grabbed him by the wrist. "That's terrible."

Craig glanced down at her hand holding his arm. He didn't hate it. "Yeah, um, but what really got me on the topic was our adoption. I have a teenage daughter, and we wound up bringing her cousin home from Austria. She's the same age as my daughter, and there's this different energy in the house now that wasn't there before."

Chelsea kept her hand on his arm. "You're a single dad to two teenage girls now? My goodness, that must be a challenge."

He nodded in response and allowed himself to relax a little with her. "It definitely is. It comes with its own challenges and problems, but we all work together to figure it out as we go along. My show talks about those issues, and it's a nice way to communicate to other families going through stuff like this that they're not alone, you know?"

She smiled again. He couldn't help but notice her lovely figure. She wore a form-fitting dress adorned with pink flowers and a white cardigan over it.

Chelsea caught him looking at her. "Yeah, this isn't normally how I dress." She tugged at the skirt. "I have to stay on-brand, you know? I wear these kinds of outfits on the show, and I wanted to be recognizable as I walked through here."

"No, you look great." Craig's stomach twisted a little as he said that. He shook off the nervousness. "I don't really have a brand since I only do audio."

For the next hour, the two of them had a few beers together and talked as the crowd at the hotel bar began to thin. Before they knew it, the time was after eleven.

"Holy cow, I can't believe it's this late already," Craig said when he looked at his watch.

"Time flies when you're having fun." She spoke with a more than flirty tone.

He looked into her eyes. *She is really cute. And she seems into me. This is so weird. I haven't been in this position in decades. I don't know what to do here.*

His nervousness finally got the better of him and Craig

finished his beer and stood from the barstool. "Well, I should get back to my room. It was really nice to meet you."

"Oh...do you want to walk together? I'm up on the sixth floor. I could ride with you."

"No, I… um…I forgot that I have to call my daughter before she goes to bed tonight. She's probably still up, and I'll have to call her the second I get into the elevator. But hey, I'll probably see you around, right? Thanks for talking to me tonight. Goodnight!"

He virtually scampered out of the bar, leaving Chelsea confused and alone to finish her beer before she headed back to her room as well. He power-walked to the elevator and ascended to the fifth floor.

By the time he turned the corner to head to his room, he glanced back to make sure nobody had followed him. He didn't know why he did that.

Once he closed the door securely, he sat on his bed and shook his head. *She hasn't even been gone a full year yet. You have so many other responsibilities and concerns on your plate right now. Why would you even entertain the thought of someone else?*

I'm sorry, Carol. I don't know what got into me down there. Maybe I'm lonely tonight, I don't know. It didn't mean anything. I was simply talking to someone. That's it. Don't think anything of it. You're still the love of my life, and I miss and love you very much.

With that, he turned the TV on, hoping to find an old sitcom from the nineties to get his mind off of the woman at the bar.

CHAPTER FIFTEEN

Vickie slammed cabinet doors one-by-one as she rifled through the remaining food in the house.

In the living room, Alexis shook her head, picked up the remote, and turned up the volume on the TV. "Hey, do you want to keep it down in there? I can't hear the TV."

"Sorry." She ran her fingers through her hair and walked into the living room. "There's no food left. I'm hungry."

"Again? We ate dinner a short while ago. And it's only Friday. We have two more days until Dad comes home. How can we be out of food?" Alexis lowered the volume on the TV again and looked at her in confusion.

"I don't know. I ate it all, I guess." She shrugged innocently. "There wasn't that much."

Her sister closed her eyes. "Vickie, what's gotten into you? Why are you eating so much?"

She sighed. "I wish I knew. I'm hungry all the time."

"Is this a vampire thing?"

"I don't remember vampires having to eat this much. At least, not in my family."

Alexis glanced out the window. "It's dark out, so it's not exactly a safe time to go out. But if we're out of food and you won't make it until the morning, I suggest you take some of that cash you earned cleaning the house and run to the pharmacy store. Stock up on a few things."

Vickie raised her eyebrows. "Are you sure? You guys always told me to never go out this late. You said it wasn't a great neighborhood."

"It's a terrible neighborhood, actually. But you're an overpowered vampire with super-speed and strength, and you can sense when you're in danger. I think you'll be fine. Try to stop and start somewhere you won't be noticed, and you can be there and back in no time."

She nodded. Alexis was right. If anyone could go out in this neighborhood after dark, it was her. As long as she moved quickly enough, she wouldn't be in any real danger.

Her mind made up, she slipped on a pair of shoes and a jacket. "Do you need anything?"

The other girl shook her head. "As long as you bring food back, I'm good. Ring the doorbell when you get here. I'll lock the doors while you're gone since I'll be home alone."

"You got it." The vampire turned and walked out the side door into the crisp, cool night. She paced in the driveway for a moment and took deep breaths to build the energy needed to burst.

She walked to the edge of the driveway and looked both ways. *No one is around. That's a good start.*

After another deep breath, she bolted from the end of

the driveway to the corner of the intersection next to the pharmacy store. *There. Now you can walk in and not be noticed at all.* She sauntered across the street and entered the store.

I've never actually been grocery shopping on my own before. She grabbed a cart and pushed it down the aisle until she reached the food section. Within minutes, she had a cart full of potato chips, boxes of cereal, a couple of gallons of milk, two loaves of bread, and a few other assorted snacks and meals.

Vickie stood back to survey her haul. *That ought to do it. It's enough to get me through the weekend.* The hairs on the back of her neck prickled and she paused, her gaze fixed blankly on the food. *What was that? Something's happening.*

Her stomach sank. *Please don't get into trouble. Please. I don't want to deal with this at the moment. I'm out here alone at night. All I want is to get home without a problem.*

Regardless of her mental dialogue, the twisting pain in her stomach told her danger was near. She looked around the store and even glanced at the overhead mirrors that gave her a comprehensive view but still saw nothing that looked remotely alarming.

A few customers walking through the aisles and one or two stock boys filled the shelves, but none of them presented as a threat. *Maybe my instincts are a little off since I'm in a different world than I used to be. I shouldn't have false alarms like this.*

Shaking her head, she pushed the cart to the front of the store and stood in line at the register. She smiled politely at the man in front of her, who was waiting his turn. He huddled into a dark-gray hooded sweatshirt with the hood pulled up. *He must be really chilly. Maybe he's here to buy cold medicine or something.*

Once the woman in front of them finished checking out, the man stepped up to the cashier and pulled his hands out of the pocket in the front of his shirt. He held a gun.

"Don't make any foolish mistakes." His hands shook with nervousness as he aimed the gun at the woman's chest. Tears filled the cashier's eyes while she froze. "Open the register and step back. And I don't want to see you pushing any emergency buttons, either. Just open the register and step back, all right?"

The girl nodded. With one hand in the air, she pushed the button to open the register and took a few steps back as he had instructed.

The man leaned over, grabbed the stacks of paper bills out of the register, and stuffed them into the pockets of his pants. A few dollars scattered free and floated slowly to the floor.

He turned and pointed the gun at everyone as he backed out of the exit to a waiting vehicle outside.

The cashier fell to her knees in terror and sobbed loudly. Vickie, however, kept her gaze trained on the man and the vehicle. As soon as they began to drive away, she walked away from her full cart and out the exit to the parking lot.

She reached the outside and heard sirens in the distance. *Somebody else must have called the police from another part of the store.* She scanned the area and saw the car—a 1989 Acura Legend in navy-blue—and knew she would follow the criminals.

What do I do when I reach them, though? I need to think fast,

*or the window to run will be gone. Once the cops are here, I have
to stay put.*

The vampire burst into a full-speed pursuit, leaped over
parked cars, and veered around big buildings. When she
caught up with the getaway car, she caught hold of the rear
of the vehicle and pushed it to the left, forcing it to collide
with a light pole.

Inside, the two criminals screamed when they lost
control. The impact was so great that both were knocked
unconscious. They were only two blocks away from the
store.

Still operating at top speed, Vickie rushed back to the
store and stopped outside the entrance. She walked in
seconds before the lights of the police cars flashed brightly
as they drew into the parking lot. Thankfully, she had
made it in time.

She sauntered back to her place but noticed the
onlookers give her strange looks. "Sorry, I had to get a shot
at the license plate number."

Once the officers arrived, they began to question those
present and one stepped up to her. "I tried to get their
license plate number, but they were already gone. Instead,
they crashed into a light pole two blocks from here. I saw
them do it when I ran outside."

Two officers looked at each other somewhat skeptically
but hurried outside to verify that her story was true. The
car remained on the side of the road, almost wrapped
around a light pole, and the two criminals were still
unconscious inside.

While they were doing that, Vickie's stomach rumbled,
and she began to feel nauseous. She jogged to the food

aisle, snatched two boxes of microwave popcorn off the shelf, and returned to toss them into her cart. "Am I able to check out now?"

One of the store managers came to the front of the store and told her to take the food. "We'll bag it for you," he said, "since you did such an excellent job taking charge of the situation and collecting information that would help the officers find the criminals. We appreciate that here."

You have no idea how much I took charge of this situation, buddy. She thanked him and walked outside once again.

Two officers stood on the pavement and stared at the damaged vehicle while they discussed what might have happened to cause the accident. When their backs were turned, she tapped into her speed once more and sprinted home.

She was so distracted by everything that had happened that she almost broke the side door. Thankfully, before she threw all her strength behind it, she remembered to ring the doorbell. Seconds later, Alexis threw the door open and looked at all the bags she carried.

"Geez, did you leave any food for the other shoppers?"

The vampire stepped into the house. "We have to turn the news on."

"Why? Are you on it?"

"Not necessarily." She was deliberately coy, which was something Alexis didn't care for. Still, she turned the TV on in time to see a report of an armed robbery attempt that took place on Teutonia Avenue.

"Why are we watching this?" Alexis shook her head.

Vickie pointed to the TV. "Because this is me."

The news anchor wore a suitably solemn expression.

"Good evening. Tonight, an armed robbery went terribly wrong for a pair of criminals. According to eyewitnesses, Rob Quigley and Ethan Cross were responsible for the theft from the registers of the Walgreens store, as well as aiming at and threatening employees and onlookers with a gun of some kind.

"However, in the middle of their escape, the duo crashed into a light pole on the side of the road, creating a gift-wrapped present for local police officers to arrive and arrest them."

"You did this?"

Vickie burst into a huge belly laugh. "I sure did. They did wrong, so I wanted to set it right."

"And you didn't get caught?"

"Nope." She beamed with pride. "I worked around all of them. Plus, I scored all this free food. You can't beat that. Here—have a bag of chips and let's relax. I'm starving more than you could ever know."

Alexis didn't argue. The vampire could out-eat anyone she knew. She couldn't understand why yet, but she knew that she and Craig needed to hash things out and clarify the expectations before she ate them out of house and home.

CHAPTER SIXTEEN

The next morning, Vickie stood at the patio door and stared at the field behind the house. Beyond the outstretched flat land, which was now brown from the mud beneath the melted snow, tall trees lined the far edge.

Being bored and stuck in the house, Vickie hadn't spent much time thinking about those trees. *I climbed some of them a few times, but that's about it. I wonder what's back there.*

She turned and walked into the living room, where Alexis was sprawled on the couch. "Aren't you bored?"

The girl looked up from the TV. "Not really. I'm enjoying the quiet, actually. This is kinda like how I spent summer vacation before you came along. I know how to deal with being bored and alone."

The vampire paced restlessly. "Well, I'm getting anxious. I want to do something, not simply sit here all weekend."

"You can do whatever you want." Alexis pulled herself into a seated position. "Nobody is stopping you. Last night, you took out armed burglars, so I don't know that there's much else that can threaten you."

Vickie gestured behind her with her thumb. "What's really in those woods back there?"

"In the field? Nothing. Well, I haven't been back there, but I've never seen anything come out of there. When we first moved in and I was little, before they flattened the whole field and leveled it, there was a dump. Like, a couple of times a week, big dump trucks would lumber across and empty their loads. But when they finished all the work, they left the trees, I guess."

"You've never been back there?" She shook her head. "How could you live here this long and have never explored a little?"

Alexis shrugged. "I don't know. I've never felt compelled to. But go ahead if you want. I don't think there's anything back there. Have fun."

After changing into a pair of jeans and a long-sleeved t-shirt, Vickie walked out the patio door and closed it behind her. Her sister shuffled through the kitchen and paused to watch her stride into the field.

I think we did too much with her when we brought her over. She's never been bored before. She doesn't know how to handle it. Now, she expects activity all the time. Not me, though. I am eating up all this boredom and enjoying every last bite.

She refilled her glass of water and returned to the couch to watch TV.

Outside, Vickie strolled along the left side of the field toward the line of trees. As she did so, a small group of men carrying large mechanical equipment crossed her path.

"Oh, sorry." She paused to let them walk through.

"Excuse us, miss." One of them smiled politely at her as they continued through the field.

I wonder what those guys are up to with all that stuff. She watched them for a moment, then pressed on and reached the edge of the trees. Her mind immediately flashed the memory of sprinting across the wide space, climbing the trees, and getting her vampire energy out of her system.

"It's funny how quickly things change," she muttered as she walked into the woods. "One minute, you have no outlet for your energy and the next minute, you use it every chance you can get. At least I'm productive now."

Sunlight streamed through the trees and peeked through the branches every so often. Large piles of pine needles were scattered everywhere. The ground was soft and mushy in places, although there wasn't too much mud because it was a little higher than the field.

It's pretty out here, at least. Vickie continued her walk, but her pleasant mood was disrupted occasionally by a lost action figure protruding from the dirt or old potato chip bags that were tossed carelessly on the ground. Drug paraphernalia and other disgusting litter could be seen every few minutes.

I'm always amazed how little concern anyone here has for this beautiful little patch of land. She shook her head in disappointment.

While it was a lovely little piece of forest, the land was also nondescript. Alexis was right—there really was nothing back there. The elevation rose and fell with a few hills but other than that, it seemed rather quiet and undisturbed, apart from the garbage.

Vickie walked farther in and tried to see what was on the other side of the trees. In no time at all, she crossed a set of train tracks and found a main road, which was busy with traffic. *I guess it's not a very big forest, anyway.*

Her mind drifted to Will. The last time she'd seen him, he had disappeared into these very trees. *I wonder if he's still out here somewhere. I hated him, but I kinda wish he would come back and help set the record straight with Alexis. I'm tired of fighting with her.*

She imagined running into him hanging from a tree or even him blindsiding her and knocking her down to pick another fight. Regardless of how she thought he might do it, she could sense that he was nowhere nearby.

When she returned to the edge of the trees that faced toward home, she stopped and watched the group of men she had run into earlier. They huddled around a spot in the middle of the field.

That's close to where Will and I fought with the Circle. What are those guys up to there? She squinted her eyes to try to make out what they were doing. They appeared to be digging slowly, while two of them set up the equipment they had lugged all the way over there.

At the dig site, Jim smiled while his men uncovered layers and layers of dirt. "It's an exciting day, gentlemen." He sniffed the morning air. "It'll be beautiful out. The snow is gone and we can finally make some real progress on this stuff."

Pete extended the metal legs under his large electro-magnetic meter. "I look forward to seeing what we can find today, Jim. If we can get even a few feet down, I bet we'll find solid evidence we can use."

His colleague nodded and shoved his hands into his pockets. "I hope so. That sword was a huge win for us, but I still think there's more here. Even if this was an ancient site of supernatural activity, we could at least prove its existence. That could buy us a few more years of funding, at least."

"I think you're right." Pete nodded while he flipped a few switches. "All right, we're set up here. I have to tweak the controls a little while we dig further, but this will really tell us what we're dealing with."

"Sir..." One of the diggers pushed up onto his knees. "If we already had a reading from this area on the balloon gauges, what will this machine do differently?"

"I got this one, Pete." Jim crouched to speak to the man. "The gauges we floated on the balloons were very basic. They only measured major sources of electromagnetic activity. This machine is much more sophisticated. It can find much lower instances and can measure them in more specific increments. That's why we're digging at such a slow pace today. We don't want to accidentally disturb anything—or, heaven forbid, break something."

Pete flipped another switch and the machine hummed to life. "Yep. This baby gives us a more complete picture."

"Excuse me?"

The group turned to look at Vickie, who stood before them with a curious look on her face. "Can I ask you a question?"

Jim and Pete swapped concerned glances, but Jim nodded confidently. "Sure, sweetheart, what can we do for you?"

"Oh, I only want to know what you're looking for out

here. I live nearby and saw you guys walking around." She was concerned that they were too close to the site of their battle with the Circle and that maybe they had left some evidence behind.

He smiled at her. "We almost ran into you earlier, didn't we?" She nodded. "Sorry about that. We're actually with the...Department of Conservation. Yeah, we are here measuring the levels of different natural resources that are in the ground. We had a tip that there were some valuable elements here and thought we should investigate further."

The vampire squinted at him. She had the sense that he was lying but there was no real way to prove it. "What does that machine do?"

Jim turned. "Pete?"

"Oh, uh...this scans the soil for a variety of different materials." The two men exchanged a smug smile for thinking so cleverly on the spot. "Yeah, that's why there are all these different gauges here."

Vickie stepped forward. "That's really interesting." As she moved, the gauges on the meter fired and swung wildly.

Pete grabbed the sides of the meter. "Yes, and it appears that we have found some interesting elements here, Jim."

The man nodded, knowing what he meant. "Well, miss, we are working on an exclusive government contract and we'll need your cooperation, so please give us the room that we need to work and be on your way. Thank you!" He tried to hurry her along.

She walked past the meter and leaned over to glance at it. "Okay, well, good luck with your findings." As she leaned, the meter made a loud pop and all the gauges dropped. Smoke seeped from under its plastic chassis. "It seems you better get that looked at!" She giggled as she walked away from them and headed back to the woods to wander for a little longer.

Jim rushed over to Pete's side and both men stared at the equipment. "What happened?"

Pete shook his head. "I have no idea. It looks like the meter blew. That's never happened before."

"What do you mean it blew? Is it useless now?"

"For now, yeah." Pete sighed. "It was overloaded by the electromagnetic activity in this region. But this thing can handle ten times the activity the balloon gauge could. This doesn't make sense to me."

Jim stepped away, frustrated that their work would grind to a halt again. "On the bright side," he said with a smile, "we're clearly on the right track here. We merely need something that can handle even more activity, I guess. If the balloon gauge wasn't enough proof, this thing blowing is even better. We should contact the Department immediately and let them know what happened."

"Should we stop digging, sir?" one of the men asked.

"Absolutely!" He ran over to them. "Don't uncover anything else. We need a reliable meter to help us dig, and it'll take some time to have another one sent to us."

Pete stared at the dirt. "I wonder what we're sitting on that caused the gauge to go that crazy that fast. We must be in the hotbed of supernatural activity right now."

Jim gave him a satisfied grin. "You aren't kidding. I bet we'll uncover a whole new avenue of scientific discovery in this region. We only have to pinpoint its source."

Meanwhile, its source wandered slowly through the

trees in the forest behind them, oblivious to what took place not far from her.

CHAPTER SEVENTEEN

After Vickie returned to the house, she spent the rest of the afternoon in her room, watching her giant TV and sending Facebook messages to Eric. Alexis remained on the couch in the living room, listlessly watching a variety of TV shows and movies and getting up only occasionally to get a snack.

Eric: *How's your nose?*

Vickie: *It's okay now. It hurt for a while, but once it popped back into place, the pain went away*

Eric: *That's good*

Eric: *Those girls are real jerks*

Vickie: *Yeah. Can't do anything about it though. Don't know how much more of it I can take. I hope this isn't how high school will be for the next couple of years*

Eric: *It won't. Besides, you have friends. Me, Jess, Jamie, Alexis*

Vickie: *I'm not so sure about Alexis anymore*

Eric: *Really? Aren't you two hanging out a lot this weekend?*

Vickie: *Nope. She has barely moved this entire weekend so far*

Eric: *Is she sick?*

Vickie: *No, she's just lazy. She says this is how she used to be bored during the summer, whatever that means*

Eric: *Are you two still fighting?*

Vickie: *idk? We're not hanging out like we usually do, that's for sure*

Eric: *I think you should go hang out with her now. Go watch TV with her. Something. You two can't hate each other all the time*

Vickie: *I don't hate her. I only wish she would show me a little respect*

Eric: *You want me to talk to her?*

Vickie: *No, I should. But I don't know how much things have cooled off. I'll go hang with her for a while and see what happens. Ttyl*

The vampire walked into the living room. Alexis appeared to have barely moved since the last time she saw her on the couch.

"What are you watching?" Vickie looked at the TV with confusion. She saw huge spaceships hurtling through space and images of young, handsome men firing laser guns at each other.

"It's a movie. *Star Wars.*" Her sister stuffed a few kernels of popcorn in her mouth.

"What's it about? Do you mind if I join you?"

Alexis gestured at the recliner with her hand but didn't move her gaze from the TV. "Go for it. It's kinda hard to explain. There's a big, evil dude named Darth Vader who's trying to take over the galaxy. Luke Skywalker is the guy who has to put together a team to defeat him. It's a fun movie. Old, but fun."

Vickie relaxed in the recliner, put her feet up, and watched the movie.

Ding. Her phone went off with a text message notification. She picked it up, unlocked it, and chuckled as she read the message. She typed a response and put her phone down. "Have you seen this movie before?"

"Yeah, a few times." Alexis stretched on the couch. "I don't know if I've ever actually sat and watched it straight through in one sitting. But I've seen all of it."

Ding. Vickie read another text, laughed quietly, typed a response, and put the phone down.

"It's actually from the 1970s, so it's fairly old. It's funny, because they came out with new ones, like, twenty-five years later or something, and the old ones look more real than the newer ones did."

The vampire smiled. *At least we're talking a little. Maybe we can get a little more comfortable with each other and this whole thing can blow over. Obviously, we needed some time apart. It'll be nice to not be so awkward around each other.*

Ding.

"Geez, who are you texting?" Alexis rolled over and looked at her with a frustrated expression on her face.

"Sorry. I can put it on silent if you want."

"I'm merely curious. Is it Eric? I thought you guys use Facebook for your messages."

Alexis was right. The couple messaged so often that they used Facebook to communicate so they wouldn't run out of text messages on their phone plans.

"No, it's Tricia."

Her sister sat up and leaned forward. "Tricia? From school?"

"Where else would I know somebody named Tricia from?" Vickie giggled. "Yeah, she's texting me right now."

"I didn't realize you two were getting to be such good friends."

She shrugged. "I guess we are. She's checking how things are going here since we wanted to hang out last night."

Alexis picked up the remote and paused the movie. "You what?"

"We wanted to hang out last night. That was until I remembered that we would be alone this weekend and I wouldn't have a ride. We're rescheduling it to next weekend. Probably Friday."

This news worried her sister. She knew the reputation Tricia had in school and she knew it was true. She didn't want such a bad influence hanging out with Vickie. "What are you planning on doing, then?"

Ding. "Hang on." Vickie tapped a response to Tricia and put her phone down. "Um…we haven't decided yet. We planned to go to her house last night. I guess we'll probably do that."

Alexis took a deep, concerned breath. "I don't think that's such a good idea."

Annoyance bubbled inside her. "Why not?"

"Because Tricia is…she's not like you or me."

Ding. She didn't pick her phone up. "What is that supposed to mean?"

The other girl shook her head. "Nothing, only that…she doesn't have the same upbringing."

"So what? Isn't that a good thing?" The vampire straightened in the chair. "Shouldn't we all want to hang out with people different from us?"

"Did you ever hear about Troy?" Alexis stared at her and she finally shook her head. "Troy is Tricia's brother. He's two years older than us."

"Okay." She shook her head and waited for the rest of the story.

"Don't you think it's weird that she has a brother two years older than her that you've never heard of? That would be a bad sign. He should be a senior right now. But he's not."

"What happened to him?"

"He was kicked out of school last year."

"For what?"

Alexis folded her arms and leaned back on the couch. "From what I heard, he punched a teacher in the face. He came to school drunk and picked a fight, not realizing it was his history teacher. Instant expulsion."

Vickie understood the point the girl was making but she didn't want to hear it. Tricia had been a very good friend to her in recent weeks—something her sister hadn't been. "Okay, but that was her brother, not her."

With a loud sigh, Alexis closed her eyes and shook her head slowly. "It trickles down. The brother still lives at home with her, and there is no indication that he's cleaned up. He got that from his parents. It's a bad household, and it's not a place you want to be. Seriously. She's bad news."

The vampire searched her brain for ways to justify it. She liked Tricia too much. "Maybe she simply needs better influences in her life. I'm a good person, right? I can help her."

Her companion laughed out loud. "Yeah, right."

"Excuse me?"

"Vickie, you've barely been in this century for what, ten months? You're still learning. Being put in that kind of environment is way out of your league."

She couldn't believe what she was hearing, especially after how the weekend had gone so far. "What, are you forbidding me to go hang out with Tricia?"

Alexis hated the way that sounded, so she wanted to dance around the wording. "I am not forbidding you. I'm merely telling you that this is a bad idea and I don't want you to go."

"Let me get this straight. It's okay for me to go out by myself to a store where armed criminals wave their guns around and steal from people but I can't go to a friend's house because you don't like them?"

The way she worded this made Alexis' blood boil. "You're not listening. Those are two completely different scenarios. Look, I was fine with you going to the store because I know you can handle yourself in that situation. You have a sense for when you are in physical danger. My goodness, a group of crazy people tried to attack you with some kind of magical sword and you got out of that. What would a guy with a gun do to you? This is a different kind of danger. She doesn't hurt other people, she hurts herself. And that can lead you to make decisions that would hurt yourself too."

Vickie had heard enough. "Tricia is being really nice to me. And do you know why she invited me over? Because she knows that I need a break from you. Ever since I've come here, you've controlled everything I do—how I dress, who I hang out with, and where I go on weekends. I'm trying to make a few decisions for myself, and you're trying to change them. Because you need to be in control."

Alexis stood from the couch. Her feelings were hurt. "All I've done for the last ten months is try to help you."

"I don't always need help!" Now, she stood as well and raised her voice. "I was raised to this age in a time and place when I fended for myself. I took care of myself and there were people walking through the villages chopping vampires' heads off. I did fine. What makes you think that I can't handle going to someone else's house by myself? I have to live my own life, you know."

She stormed off to her room and slammed the door shut.

Her sister sank down onto the couch and stared at the frozen image of Han Solo wielding a blaster. She thought of last summer before her mom died when she still was blessed with the ability to be bored and watch an old movie on the TV by herself.

Now, she couldn't even do that. Her mind was preoccupied with the prospect of a bad girl at school getting her vampire friend drunk or hooked on drugs.

What does a vampire do if she smokes weed? Or even a cigarette? What if she gets cornered by Troy? Will he do anything?

She rubbed her face and shook her head in frustration, trying to relax. *This is a whole lot easier with Dad here. Maybe he could talk some sense into her.*

In her bedroom, Vickie threw herself onto her bed in

anger. *She's helped me so much, but now that I need to start doing things on my own, she can't handle it. She has to have her little fingers in everything so that she can steer me. It's like I'm her project. I'm not even my own person.*

She stared at the ceiling. *At times like these, I miss the old days. I never fought with my siblings this much. We loved each other, respected each other, and we always had fun. Exactly like when I first got here. It's been less fun lately.*

I don't even know what to do about it anymore.

CHAPTER EIGHTEEN

"I'll have a whiskey sour, please." Jim sat down at the bar of the Radisson Hotel, frustrated and tired.

The bartender poured the drink and slid it in front of him. He thanked him and took a swig. As he put the glass down, he stared at it. *Am I doomed to fail at this? How many more times will things blow up—literally and figuratively— before I can make this work? At what point will they stop funding these studies?*

He leaned back and listened to the lousy local guitarist who played live music for the Saturday night crowd. *It's not exactly Nashville or Austin, but I guess it's something.*

A hand slapped him on the shoulder. He spun to see Pete climb into the stool beside him with a sympathetic smile. "How are you holding up?" He gestured to the bartender.

"About as well as our meter." Jim loved gallows humor whenever he was down.

Pete waved his hand dismissively and looked down. "Hey, it ain't over yet. We have a rush order on a different model—the MX-385. This one is even stronger than what we used. It might not be as accurate but it should hold up against any flare-ups like that. Apparently, that's the issue here in this location." The bartender stepped up and Pete ordered a beer.

"It's amazing how many different ways these things can go wrong, eh?" Jim took another swig.

"But the difference here, Jim, is this time, it went wrong in a good way. Come on, in these situations, we always deal with something going haywire and completely disproving whatever theory we're working on. It never fails. We run into some obstacle that brings everything to a grinding halt and we look like idiots."

He nodded solemnly. "Yeah, this time, at least, the equipment blew because we are so right this time." He chuckled to himself. "Even when we win, we lose."

"But we're winning. That's the important part." The bartender delivered a beer, and Pete took a sip. "There's nothing like a cold beer after a long day."

"I don't want to look at another meter right now. After staring at that thing all afternoon, my mind is burned out."

Pete nodded. "I get it. You'll have a couple days' break. We can relax and enjoy the Milwaukee scene, I guess. Like this guy jamming up there. This the best they've got?"

"I sure hope not." Jim released a belly laugh. "Ah, Pete, I'm getting impatient. This is the closest we've been, you know?"

"I do know. After the last few clunkers, I didn't think we would ever get this close." He flipped through the menu, looking for appetizers.

Jim leaned in and pointed at him with his drink in his

hand. "I tell you what, I worried that we would be another footnote in one of those history books. Like the Nazis, right? All their stuff looked ridiculous in hindsight. We'd be left to history as the secret US government agency that investigated the supernatural and never came up with anything."

Pete lifted the bottle to his lips. "How much money have we spent from our government grants?"

"I don't want to think about it." He bristled at the comment. Money made him anxious. Budgets frustrated him. He simply liked the work. "To me, each failure brought us a little closer to success. But I don't think this is the one that fails. This time, we hit the jackpot. There's something out there, man. Something happened in that field. Or will happen again. I don't know. I only know I'll be there to find out."

"Excuse me." Pete nodded to the bartender. "Are the fried cheese curds any good? I've never had them."

"Oh, Wisconsin's finest, sir." The bartender flashed a big, brilliant smile. "If you're visiting Wisconsin, you have to try the curds. With a big cup of marinara sauce."

"Let's do it. Thanks." He turned to Jim. "So you'll be there. What happens if ol' Uncle Sam stops signing the checks? What then? Are you gonna do it for free?"

"I'm telling you right now, Pete, I truly, firmly believe that something is happening here in Milwaukee. Today proved that. If they stop paying me, fine. I'll get a job here and move. I'll flip burgers and bag groceries, and I'll spend every hour I'm not at work in that field trying to find out what's going on."

Pete admired his dedication to the work. In some ways,

he envied it. With his wife and kids at home in Virginia, he couldn't throw himself into the work like Jim could. It was both good and bad at the same time.

"You know they run out of patience at some point, right?"

Jim scoffed. "Of course. That's what happened with the Ghost Plane in 2003."

The Ghost Plane was an odd phenomenon in the fall of 2003 that nobody could explain to that day. A plane landed at an independent airport in Tacoma, Washington. It could hold four people on board, but it wasn't scheduled to land there.

Pete shook his head as he thought about it. "That might have been my favorite mystery, and I only wish we had more time to decipher it. Man, the plane lands there out of nowhere—no one knows where it came from—and the propellers run for what, twenty minutes?"

"Twenty minutes, yep." Jim nodded and smiled wistfully as he recalled the case. "No one got out or radioed anyone from inside the plane. Everyone simply sat there and stared at the thing for almost half an hour. Once the propellers stopped, they opened it and no one was on board."

The bartender brought a basket of small fried cheese curds with a cup of marinara sauce spilling over the side. They thanked him and let the basket rest for a moment to cool.

"My favorite part of that story"—Pete gestured with his index finger—"is the parachutes. All four parachutes were there so no one jumped out. There was no evidence of anyone being there, either. They had the plane surrounded. No one would have gotten away without being seen." He laughed. "The Ghost Plane. Man, that was fun."

Jim grabbed one of the curds and dipped it in the marinara sauce. "But think of the implications of that. Either we have a plane that can fly and safely land itself, or—"

"Ghost pilots." Pete cackled.

"You laugh, but outfit our Air Force with either of those and the ways we can fight wars transform before our very eyes, right? It's huge. It's the coolest achievement in military history and could've saved countless lives." He popped the cheese curd in his mouth and bit into it. "Oh, my goodness, these are delicious."

"Let me try one." Pete took a bite. "Wow! How do we get these at home?"

The bartender walked past and laughed. "It's a Wisconsin thing, boys. It's never the same anywhere else."

"Anyway"—Pete shifted on his barstool—"we couldn't crack it. That's the problem with investigating the supernatural. You need conclusive proof, especially if we intend to plan military missions based on this stuff. We couldn't get that proof with the Ghost Plane. We sunk six months into that plane, with no result."

Jim held his whiskey sour up to his chin. "Yep. After all that, we still couldn't prove it. It became a story of legend that no one can explain. Everyone thought we were crazy."

"I thought they would shut down the department after that one. I really did." Pete snagged a few more curds.

"You thought that would bring this to an end? No way. For me, 2008 was the year I thought we were done."

Pete drew his eyebrows together. "Which one 2008?"

"The Neverending Army?"

"Oh, man…"

The Neverending Army was the code name for an investigation into the apparent claims of a man who offered proof that he'd reanimated a dead frog.

"Do you remember that dude's name?" Pete laughed. "What a crackpot he turned out to be."

"Stanley Ignatowski!" Jim snapped his fingers.

"Yes! Stanley! I cannot believe we had him under our wing for almost the entire year."

Jim thought back to the investigation. Ignatowski had injected a proprietary fluid into a dead frog and brought it back to life. He would make these claims repeatedly, and there was enough evidence to prove that he had successfully done it.

"The zombie army." He stared at nothing in particular for a moment. "You talk about changing the face of war? Bringing soldiers back to life after they died in battle? Now that's changing a military strategy! We wouldn't have to draft people anymore. We could lower our numbers dramatically. As long as we kept the soldiers intact…"

"Yeah, but Stanley was out of his mind." Pete took another sip of beer. "He couldn't replicate the success, but we continued to push the investigation forward."

"That got messy really quickly. But still, I believed in that guy. I thought he could pull it off. He was living proof that supernatural activity could occur." He believed what he was saying, even though the entire investigation failed.

"You couldn't get him to do it successfully on a human." Pete almost shouted in amusement. "The only reason we kept Stanley around that long was because you believed it so much."

Jim scooped up a handful of cheese curds. "But this is it, Pete. None of those failures matter anymore. None of the cut funding, none of the experiments that went nowhere, and none of the investigations that failed. That's all in the past. We have repeatable proof that something in that field was supernatural. There is a being somewhere in Milwaukee that caused that. We'll get our hands on it and we'll learn its strengths, weaknesses, everything…and we'll use it for our own good."

"Do you worry about anyone going out there? What about that girl?" Pete looked into Jim's eyes. "She was a little too curious for my comfort."

He pursed his lips. "I doubt it. It's a field in the middle of nowhere, and it serves a function. It's a flood basin. No one hangs out down there. And for now, the girl was merely a passerby. She had good timing, that's all. If it turns out we're drawing too much attention, maybe we can think of a way to conceal it better. But for now, we're safe."

There was a beat of silence.

"Do you really think this is it?" Pete asked. "Do you think this is what everything has been leading to for decades? Are you willing to put your career on the line to bring this one home?"

"Pete, I'm willing to put my life on the line for this one. Every other investigation we've done in this department has been based on hearsay and witnesses. This is the first and only time we've been able to accurately and precisely measure supernatural activity. I don't care what I have to do—who I have to hurt or step over, if necessary—to bring whatever this being is back to Washington DC with me. I won't go back to that office without someone or something coming along with me."

The other man took a deep breath. "It might be the last thing you ever do. Even if you find it, there's no proof you can control it."

He smiled. "I'll control it. And I'll use it to our advantage. By any means necessary, I will make this my hallmark success—and everyone and everything will be forced out of my way to make that happen."

Pete hated it when Jim talked like that. It made him uncomfortable. He took another swig of his beer to calm his nerves, then changed the topic of conversation to the terrible guitar player on the other side of the room.

CHAPTER NINETEEN

The audience erupted into applause after Joe Rogan finished his presentation to the conference and walked off the stage. The entire room buzzed with energy.

Craig looked at the man who sat beside him. "That guy is full of enthusiasm. It makes me want to go take on the world."

The man laughed. "A dangerous combination of standup comedian and MMA enthusiast. He has tons of adrenaline pumping through his body and he knows how to use it." He wished him well and walked in the other direction after they stood from their seats.

Craig's smile fell. He hadn't exactly made any friends at this conference. He did his best, but he was so far out of his element that he felt handcuffed whenever he tried to interact with anyone he didn't know.

Nodding with something close to resignation, he turned to his right and slid out of the row of seats. *That was a great presentation, though. I feel like we're already doing most of what he talked about—being ourselves, being honest, and getting to the truth. That's basically what we're working on, and I think that's why the podcast is doing so well.*

It was midday, and many people headed out to get lunch. He decided he would go to his room and order room service—not because he didn't want to go out but because he was in a fancy hotel and wanted to see what the room service was like for the upper crust.

Because of that, he was able to hang back in the hotel and explore some of the booths without pushing and shoving his way through the massive crowd. As the population thinned, the casual observer could really spend time with some of the products and services on offer without fear of holding up the lines.

As he walked into the hall of booths, he saw Chelsea on the other side of the room. She looked beautiful. Her long, curly red locks were gathered into a sloppy bun and she wore a green floral-print dress and a gray cardigan over the top. It was cute and beautiful at the same time, and he couldn't help but stare. *She looks even better in the daylight than she did in the dim light of the bar.*

But once he recognized that she was there, he spun and left the hall and waited outside the doors for a few minutes. He nodded and smiled at a few people as they walked past in an effort to look natural, even though he felt anything but.

This is stupid. You can't stop participating in this expensive conference because you're embarrassed around one woman. Get back in there. You can work around her.

He slipped back through the doors and peered carefully down the line of booths. Chelsea lingered at a booth promoting a new video camera system, so he walked quickly around the long way so he could move past her without being seen. That would enable him to make his way down to the other end of the booths and work his way back. *Maybe by the time I get to the front again, she'll be out to lunch.*

Craig turned his attention to a booth with a large banner labeled, *PhoneCast.*

"Sir, are you in the audio podcast world?" A young man with shoulder-length hair and a wispy goatee greeted him.

"Yes, I am." *There you go. Get yourself back in the game and grow some confidence. You're comfortable here. These are your people.*

"Then I would love to introduce you to PhoneCast. It's an app that takes all the complicated technical difficulties of podcasting and condenses them into a few different easy-to-use options. All you have to do is open your phone and press the record button, and our app does all the heavy lifting. It even publishes the podcast for you."

See? Aren't you glad you came down this way? Now this is the kind of service you could see yourself using. "This is really interesting. I'd love to hear some examples of how well these types of recordings sound in real life compared to a professional setup."

"So would I." Craig instantly recognized the voice behind him. His stomach leaped into his throat.

He turned to greet her. "Chelsea, good to see you again." *Don't lay it on too thick, man. She'll see right through that. Just be polite.* "What brings you over here? I thought you were down at the other end."

She smirked knowingly and cocked an eyebrow. "You

saw me down there and decided to move to the opposite end of the hall, hey?"

He flushed involuntarily with embarrassment. "No…I… See, I had already planned to start on this side. In fact, I was halfway to this booth before I turned and looked back and thought, *Oh, Chelsea's here, I'll have to catch up with her later. I'm already this far.*" He knew he was rambling, but he couldn't stop himself.

Fortunately for him, she did. "It's okay. I'm only teasing you. No, I saw the sign for this one and I wanted to see what it was all about."

"Yeah, but you do video shows, right?" He tried to reign in his awkwardness and act natural. "This is for audio podcasts."

"I know. But the more people I meet here who have audio shows, the more I think I should do something in that space. What do you think?" She tilted her head and gave him an inquisitive look that made him completely forget the conversation for a split second.

"Well, um…you wouldn't have to worry about what you wore." *That's the best you could do? Be more awkward, Craig. Good grief.*

She giggled. "You're right about that."

The two of them stood side by side as they listened to the PhoneCast app founder make his presentation. They walked away intrigued by the technology, and Craig wondered aloud if it was something that he could use.

"Do it only if it'll save you time." Chelsea knew her stuff, apparently. "You're a small operation, and implementing a new technology is only worthwhile if it'll pay off. Don't change your routine simply because it seems cool."

"That's a good point. You know, you have a good head on your shoulders." He glanced at her and she met his gaze with a smile.

"You can't run your own business without at least some brains. Or, at least, the ability to outsource the brainy stuff." They both laughed. "But I don't outsource. I like having control over my own thing."

Craig nodded. "I do, too. That was one of the unexpected surprises about doing this. I find I really love having that control."

She averted her eyes for a moment as if she were a little shy. She stopped walking and turned to face him. "I had a really nice time last night."

"Me too." His palms began to sweat.

"I have a hard time making friends here. I'm a little shy. Finding someone who's easy to talk to is huge. It was such a relief to relax and laugh without worrying about networking or anything like that." She tried to lead him to the same conclusion she was making, but she didn't want to have to say it out loud.

"I know what you mean. It was great to simply swap stories over a drink and not worry about anything else. Sometimes, you get so wrapped up in all the conference stuff that you forget you're a person, not merely a brand!" He laughed politely at his own little joke.

"So...what are you doing tonight?" She gave him a hopeful look.

"Tonight?" He raised his eyebrows nervously.

"Yeah. Instead of meeting at the hotel bar, maybe we could...I don't know, find some dinner somewhere? There are restaurants in every direction. I actually saw a cool Italian place on the other side of the block. Do you like pasta?" She smiled warmly again in a way that almost melted him.

Craig put his hands on his hips awkwardly and looked at the floor. "Um...tonight won't work. I can't. Yeah, I... have to check in with my daughter. Daughters, I guess. I haven't talked to them since I left and I want to make sure the house is still in one piece, you know what I mean?" He laughed uncomfortably and tried to ignore the obvious disappointment in her face. "I tried last night but they'd obviously already gone to sleep. It's the perils of father-hood. Those girls are my life and I have to make sure they're okay, even when I'm away."

"No, I get it. That's okay. I guess...maybe some other time? The next conference?" He nodded and she turned to walk away.

She sighed quietly while she walked. Craig watched her intently, and with every step she took, he felt worse and worse. Finally, he hurried after her and tapped her on the shoulder. "Chelsea... Look, I'm sorry."

"No, *I'm* sorry." She smirked. "I thought we had a little spark last night, that's all. I wanted to see where it would go. Maybe I read you wrong or something. It's okay but I'm a little embarrassed. Don't mind me." Her cheeks glowed pink.

"No, no, there's nothing to be embarrassed about. There was a spark. I felt it too. But...I don't know. I haven't been single for that long, and with my girls at home, I'm not sure if—"

She held her hand up. "It's okay. I understand. You're still going through so much. Your wife hasn't been gone for very long, and you are still trying to learn how to live."

"Exactly." In a way, he was relieved that she could articulate what he was trying to say.

"I don't want to pressure you. If you change your mind and you decide to grab a bite tonight with no expectations at all, I'm happy to join you. If not, that's okay too. But I'll promise you now that you have a new fan. I'll listen to your podcast. And if you ever decide you're interested or ready, you can look me up."

She smiled and walked away, and Craig decided it was a good time to go back to his room and order lunch.

The entire walk and elevator ride up to the fifth floor was loaded with anxiety. *I really like her. She's so cool and cute and seems really into me. But is that okay?*

He walked into his room and located the room service menu. While he held it, he glanced at his left hand where his wedding ring used to rest.

It's so funny, Carol. I used to think I would wear that ring for the rest of my life. I thought I'd be buried with it on. Instead, I gave it back to you. And without it, I don't know how to handle myself in any of these situations.

I don't know what's right, what's okay, or what's even good for me. I haven't had to do this for so long. I always appreciated your advice. I wish you were here to give it. Of course, if you were here, then I wouldn't need your advice about this particular topic.

Either way, I still wish you were here. Life is so much more complicated without you.

CHAPTER TWENTY

Vickie stayed in her room for the rest of the evening. She couldn't even stand to look at Alexis.

When she walked to the bathroom to brush her teeth and get ready for bed, she was so angry about the situation that her fangs actually protruded a little. *This is ridiculous. Why am I so upset by this? I'm not in physical danger.*

She took a few deep breaths after brushing her teeth and hair, then walked out of the bathroom and past Alexis, who was on her way to bed. They avoided eye contact, and the tension hung in the air.

The vampire closed her bedroom door behind her and leaned against it. Holding her tongue on the tip of one of her fangs, she closed her eyes and regained control of her emotions to retract them.

Once that was done, she turned the lights off and crawled into her bed.

The streetlight beyond the front lawn was shining through the window and cast shadows on the ceiling that distracted her briefly. *Remember what it was like to be inde-*

pendent and respected by your family? Those were the good old days, I guess.

Wait...I can remember those moments whenever I want.

Vickie closed her eyes and concentrated. Her mind took her back four hundred years to Salzburg. When she opened her eyes, she stood in the middle of the village square.

Why did I come here?

Chickens clucked as they scurried on the dirt paths. People hawked their produce and stands filled with apples, pears, and other juicy fruits lined the path. Villagers pushed and shoved their way through. Everyone had dirt smudged on their faces as it was almost impossible to stay perfectly clean.

She took a few steps, bewildered as to why she was placed in this particular memory. Although she enjoyed the familiarity of the village and its people, that single moment didn't ring any bells for her.

A sniffling sound caught her attention.

Her gaze scanned the area and finally settled on a little girl seated near a water pump, her face in her hands. The child's long black hair covered her fingers and hung down in front of her face.

Vickie approached the girl, who lowered her hands and looked up. *Oh, goodness, it's me. I don't remember this at all. What is so upsetting?*

Little Victoria looked around at the people walking past with puffy, bloodshot eyes, her bottom lip curled in grief. All the vampire wanted to do was comfort the poor girl, even though it was herself.

She walked around the pump and stared at the shadow

of her childhood as she tried to determine the reason for the problem.

I'm not in any kind of physical pain. I'm not grieving over anything. I'm scared. But what am I scared of? What worried me so much in this moment that I let go of my inhibitions and cried openly and publicly? That's not like me at all.

Time ticked by while she sat and watched herself as she tried to find answers. Young Victoria drew her knees up to her chest and hugged them tightly as if she tried to make herself as small as possible.

"Victoria!" Vickie knew that sound.

A smile spread across her face as her father burst onto the scene. *It is always so wonderful to see him in the flesh, even if I'm not actually here.*

He found Young Victoria and scrambled over to comfort her. Without a word, he wrapped his big, burly arms around her and pulled her close to his chest. As he stroked her hair, he nodded and repeated over and over, "You're okay. Vater is here."

Vickie walked up and crouched beside him, wishing she could wrap her arms around him. But since he was only a shadow, all she could do was watch.

"I'm so sorry, my daughter." He brushed the hair away from her tear-soaked cheeks. "Your siblings will not escape punishment."

My siblings? What did they do? Did they hurt me? That doesn't sound like them. They must be the reason I am crying, but that doesn't jog any memories for me.

Her father scooped Young Victoria up in his arms and held her tightly, and the two of them made their way to the edge of the village. Vickie knew exactly what he was doing, so she rushed to keep up with them. *You can't reveal yourself, Vater. You'd better get outside of town before you tap into that super-speed.* She smiled knowingly.

Once they were a safe distance from the village and out of eyesight, Vickie began to build up her energy levels—which, in this dreamlike state, fired instantly. She burst into speed alongside her father and the younger version of herself who now held on for dear life by gripping her father's overcoat.

They reached the castle, and she followed them eagerly inside. Her father carried Young Victoria up to her bedroom and assured her that everything was okay now.

"You are home and you are safe. I will deal with your siblings." He walked out of the room and shut the door.

Again with the talk about my siblings. What did they do to me? Why was I crying?

That question lingered in her mind, but she also had something else to consider—Young Victoria's mindset. She could sense that the little girl she was watching was still very upset. She had no idea why, but she could definitely understand the targets of her rage.

Vickie sat on the edge of her childhood bed and watched her younger self intently as she cleaned herself up and brushed her hair. *I am furious at my brother and sister. Look at me bare my teeth. I am ready to kill them. The hair on my arms and the back of my neck is standing up. Little girl, what did they do to you?*

She had zero memory of this incident, and she was fascinated by the rage that coursed through the body of herself as a young child.

But before she could explore any farther, both Vickies heard a loud wail coming from downstairs.

The vampire raced past the younger version of herself, who remained hidden in the bedroom. The wails came from her mother, and she was in the kitchen.

When she arrived, her father clasped her mother in his arms and held her upright to keep her from collapsing. *Is Mutter sick? She looks like she is ready to collapse.*

She moved closer and noticed tears in her father's eyes. *Those are tears of grief. Oh no.*

Vickie put two and two together in her head, and she immediately knew what moment she had transported back to. A lump formed in her throat as she watched the crippling pain in her parents' eyes as they processed the news for the first time.

"Where were they?" her mother asked between blubbery sobs.

"We found them in a barn. The Circle appears to have gotten to them." Her father could barely choke the words out through his gritted teeth.

The poor woman wailed louder, knowing exactly what he meant by that. Vickie sat on a stool and leaned against the wall as she watched it unfold. *They wouldn't tell me that day what happened. They chose to wait to break the news to me. But my mom knows in this moment that her son and daughter were both beheaded. I never really thought about the pain this caused them.*

Much like he'd grasped Young Victoria's shoulders and assured her of safety, Vickie's father held her mother by her shoulders and looked into her eyes. "My dear wife, this is a time for us to be strong in the face of fear. Victoria needs to know that everything will be okay."

"But how will everything be okay?" her mother pleaded through her tears. "How can we say that to her? Almost half of our family is gone because of them."

He nodded solemnly and choked his tears back. "I don't know yet. But we cannot live in fear. That is no life. We need to comfort her with the knowledge that, although her siblings are gone, we are still here. She is still here. Life needs to continue."

Overwhelmed by the emotions of the moment, Vickie stood and returned to Young Victoria in her bedroom. Despite the wailing from the kitchen, the girl still held onto her rage for her brother and sister, and Vickie could not understand why.

You poor girl, you're about to be all alone. What is so important that you must be so angry at them? You don't even know they are gone. Of course, despite her pleading thoughts, she could not communicate anything to the younger version of herself.

Instead, she watched in shock as her shadow stalked around the room and plotted to bring harm to her two siblings who were now unknowingly deceased.

Then came the knock at the door.

Vickie's stomach twisted in knots, full of nervousness over what she was about to witness. *I don't remember any of this. Why don't I remember any of this?*

Her father walked in and closed the door. He sat on Victoria's bed and patted the place beside him, urging her to sit with him. With a deep breath, he took his young daughter by the hand and told her that her siblings were both dead.

"But how?"

"They were…in an accident, my dear. They were hurt too badly to recover in time. Neither of them was strong enough."

Tears welled in the little girl's eyes, but she didn't cry or sob. She simply stared off into space, slack-jawed. The shock of the moment had frozen her.

Her father held her tightly and struggled to keep his composure. "This is okay. You will be okay. We will be okay. We are still a family—your mother, you, and me." He released her, and she straightened to look at him. "I will leave you to your grief. But please, please come speak with me or your Mutter if you need anything at all, my flower. Please talk to us."

"Yes, Vater."

He left the room but paused in the doorway to gaze upon his remaining child one more time before he left.

Why don't I remember this?

Vickie watched her younger self stare off into space again. Tears dripped down her cheeks, but she didn't sob or scream.

She could sense that there was more than grief inside the child. She sat next to the little girl and tried to listen to what she was feeling.

Then, her eyes snapped open. She was back in her bed in the twenty-first century, staring at the shadows on the ceiling.

"It was guilt," Vickie whispered as the realization came. "I blocked that memory out because I felt guilty. I was so angry at my siblings for whatever they did to me, and it was never resolved because they died before we could address it. I felt guilty that I had hated them so much while they were dying somewhere."

She sat in her bed and pulled her knees up. "Oh, that poor girl. You couldn't handle the grief and the guilt, so you pushed it away. You held onto your anger, and it was too late to do anything about it. They died unforgiven by you, and it crushed you."

CHAPTER TWENTY-ONE

The sun rose on Sunday morning and Vickie rolled out of bed. It wasn't the most relaxing night of sleep she'd ever had, and she blinked her eyes repeatedly to try to will herself awake.

Throughout the night, she woke up every couple hours with her siblings on her mind. *How could I have been so angry at them?*

She pulled on a sweatshirt and a pair of sweatpants and shuffled into the kitchen. To her surprise, Alexis was scrubbing dishes.

"Morning."

"Morning." The other girl didn't turn to look at her. The water in the sink splashed as she wiped dried food off a plate.

"What are you doing?" She had expected Alexis to be lying in the living room, if awake at all.

"What's it look like? I'm doing the dishes."

Her curt tone was not lost on Vickie. "Okay, but why?"

Alexis chuckled and shook her head. "Is this a trick

question? My dad is on his way home this morning and the house is messy. I'm trying to clean it up before he gets here so we don't get in trouble."

The vampire walked up behind her and looked over her shoulder. "I thought I was in charge of the cleaning. You know, because I can do it faster."

"I didn't know when you would be awake, so I thought I would do it myself. It's no big deal. It needs to be done."

Vickie gave her a nudge. "I'll do it. I can have it done in a few seconds and then we don't have to worry about it."

"No, really, it's fine."

"Come on, I want to help."

"You're not helping, you're only getting in my way and slowing me down now."

She was determined not to take no for an answer. Rather than make a verbal protest, she reached around Alexis and tried to pick up one of the plates that were in the sink.

Her sister yanked it out of her hands. "Let me do this, okay?"

Vickie pulled her hand back. "Alexis, don't pick a fight with a vampire."

Alexis dropped the plate in the sink and turned to her with her eyebrows raised. "Is that some kind of threat? Now you're threatening me?"

"No." She sighed. "This isn't going the way I wanted it to. I only want to help." The guilt over her siblings still bubbled inside her.

"I'll clean up. You can go watch TV."

"No chance. Give me the plate." She snatched the plate again and sparked a tug of war between the two girls.

"Knock it off!"

With one jerk, the plate slipped free and flipped out of their hands onto the kitchen floor, where it shattered into dozens of little pieces. The surprise of the impact jolted both girls into silence.

"Oh, great." Alexis shook her head. "Now we have a real mess to clean up before Dad gets home."

Vickie raised her palms. "Don't worry about it. I'll finish the dishes, then I'll get the vacuum and clean this up, okay?"

Tired of fighting, the other girl nodded and walked around the shattered plate on the way to her room.

That's fine. Stay in your room for a while and cool off. I'll take care of things out here.

Before she closed her bedroom door, Alexis called out: "Run the vacuum through the whole place, then. Dad will notice if we don't." She closed the door.

Vickie looked at the pile of dishes next to the sink and inhaled sharply through her nose. *You don't need a whole ton of speed for this. Only enough to move it along.*

As the energy built up, her hands moved in a flurry to scrub dishes clean and dry them with the towel. Her gaze darted constantly to make sure she did a good job.

Once all the dishes were clean and put away, she slowed and retrieved the vacuum from the front closet. She unspooled the power cord, walked to the kitchen, and plugged it in. While doing so, she glanced down the hallway at Alexis' closed bedroom door.

That's your sister in there. She's your family now. You have to find a way to get along with her and make this work. Think about how mad you were at your siblings on the day they died.

Vickie shook her head and tried to quiet those thoughts while she turned on the vacuum cleaner and primed her body for another rapid bout of cleaning. Seconds later, she whipped through the house, vacuuming each room and the hallway.

But in the seconds she spent in the kitchen, she began thinking about the memories that she accessed. *I don't know what could have been so awful that I held such anger for my sweet brother and sister. It must have been nothing, or I wouldn't have felt so guilty that I blocked the memory from my brain.*

These thoughts distracted her, but a loud clunk jolted her back to the present reality. She looked down to see the head of the vacuum cleaner broken into several pieces. The still-functioning remnants whirred and squealed loudly until she turned it off.

Vickie dropped the handle of the vacuum to the floor as Alexis stormed out of her room. "What on Earth was that sound?" She stopped in her tracks when she reached the kitchen.

It appeared that she had accidentally slammed the vacuum cleaner into the door of the refrigerator. The door dented and buckled and it fell off one of its hinges to rest partially on the floor.

The cool air of the fridge rushed out and struck Vickie in the face. She wore a spooked expression as her sister approached.

"How...how did this happen?" Alexis crouched to look at what was left of the vacuum cleaner.

"I don't know. I guess I was distracted." She stepped over to the fridge and tried to lift the door and jam it back into place, but it continued to hang off the one hinge to let the cold air escape.

Alexis sat on the floor and crossed her legs. "We're screwed. There's no way we can hide this. Dad will be home, like, any minute now and two major appliances are destroyed."

She had no idea how true her words were. Only a mile down the road, Craig drove without a care, happy to be back home. *Ah, it's nice to be somewhere familiar again. Away from the distractions, back to a routine.*

For all his contentedness, a burning frustration had lingered in his mind during the entire drive home. *All that money and the best thing I got out of the weekend was a few glorified pep talks and a whole slew of sales pitches.* His mind drifted to Chelsea. *And a dogpile of guilt. Not exactly a successful trip.*

Still, relief washed over him when he pulled into the driveway.

In the house, the girls heard the SUV draw up outside.

Vickie shook her head. "What are we going to do?"

"Nothing." Alexis shrugged. "All we can do now is take it. We have nowhere to run and nowhere to hide." She pulled herself to her feet and walked over to the kitchen table. As she sat, the side door opened.

"Where are my girls?" Craig announced as he entered the house, dragging his bag behind him. "I've waited for..." His voice trailed off as he walked into the kitchen and saw the carnage. "W-What..." He stood in place, speechless for a few moments.

"How'd it go, Dad?" Alexis asked, apparently ignoring the damage.

With his eyes bugged in disbelief, her father looked at her. "What happened here?"

"It was my fault." Vickie raised her hand. "I was vacuuming and I got distracted."

"I'll say." He dropped his bag at his feet and put his hands on his hips. "I take it you must have used your powers to clean?" She nodded. "Alexis, didn't we talk about this?"

"I had nothing to do with this, Dad."

He didn't believe her. "You have been very clear that you wanted Vickie to do the chores in the house because she can do them faster. Don't lie to me. If you were responsible for encouraging this, I want to know right now."

The vampire stepped between Alexis and her father and held her hands out. "It was me. It was all me. Alexis tried to do the cleaning this morning. I insisted that I be the one to do it. I thought it was a good idea, but I was too distracted to do it right, I guess."

"No kidding." He kicked the broken vacuum cleaner lightly. "Well, this will have to come out of your account then. You'll pay for a new vacuum and a new fridge."

Vickie winced. "How expensive is that going to be?"

"The vacuum won't be too bad—a couple of hundred bucks. The fridge, on the other hand? It'll be three times that, probably. We'll see what deals we can find. From now on, no more using your powers for household chores. If you want to clear it with me, that's fine, but not on your own. You obviously can't handle it properly, and I want to be sure that our house is safe." He pointed to his daughter. "Go downstairs and get the coolers. Bring them all up, because we need to save this food before it spoils. The fridge's motor will burn out in no time and we'll have a fridge full of spoiled food."

His daughter nodded as she walked past him and gave him a kiss on the cheek to welcome him home. "We missed you, Dad." She walked down the stairs to the basement.

"I missed you girls, too." Craig picked his bag up and tossed it onto the kitchen table. He sat in one of the chairs and sighed, tapping his fingers on the table as he stared out the window.

"Did you have a good time? Was it worth it?" Vickie stepped forward cautiously in case he was fuming with rage.

But to her surprise, he was calm. "It definitely was not worth it. There were a few cool presentations, but it's not really my thing. I don't want to network with other people, I merely want to get better at my craft. Those guys were very preoccupied with making money and all that."

She didn't understand the problem with that. "What's wrong with making money?"

He chuckled. "Nothing, unless it consumes you and it's all you ever talk about. It was simply a conference for a group of socially awkward people who tried to use the event to generate more content for their own podcasts. There wasn't much substance to anything they said."

Alexis emerged from the basement dragging two large coolers behind her. Her father stood and helped her move them to the middle of the kitchen. He pulled his junk drawer open, located a screwdriver, and removed the other hinge from the fridge so the door could be lifted free.

He opened the cheese drawer, retrieved his bag of cheese curds, and tossed it into one of the coolers. "There.

I've taken care of the important stuff. Now, it's your turn to finish this job while I unpack."

The two girls worked side by side, reluctantly being civil despite the days of bad blood between them.

And even though Vickie hated the job and wanted it over as quickly as she could, she also knew that Craig would easily tell if she used her powers.

The two of them labored on to pack various refrigerated goods into the cooler for safekeeping.

CHAPTER TWENTY-TWO

That night, despite the damage in the kitchen, the house started to look a little more normal again.

Vickie walked into the living room where Craig was seated in his recliner and Alexis sprawled on the couch with her phone.

She dropped onto the floor and placed her phone next to her, unlocked it and tapped away. After sending a message to Eric to see if he was online, she rolled to her side and looked at Craig, who sat with his laptop in his lap. "What are you working on?"

"I'm deciding how to spend your money." He gave her a wink. "I'm looking up refrigerators and trying to see if I can find a good deal without having to pay an arm and a leg."

"Hey, Dad, what if we went with stainless steel? And a fridge that has a water dispenser on the front?"

Vickie shot Alexis an excited glance. "I've seen those."

Her sister nodded. "They're awesome. Cold water on

demand, filtered, clean, straight from the fridge whenever you want."

"Let's slow down, girls. There are three reasons why that won't happen."

"I know, I know, it's too expensive." Alexis mocked her father before he had a chance to explain.

"I'll let that go." He gave her a look of warning. "Yes, number one, it's too expensive. Number two, stainless steel appliances have to match, or it looks weird. If we bought a new fridge, we'd have to buy a new oven, at least, and probably a new dishwasher and possibly a new microwave. That turns this little project into several thousand dollars of expenses."

Alexis shrugged. "It's fine by me."

"Ha-ha. Unless you both plan to pitch in, it ain't happening. Third, speaking of expenses, you can't have a fridge that dispenses water installed anywhere. It has to be near a water line. Our fridge is on the opposite side of the kitchen from the faucet. That means a new water line would have to be installed over there. Again, too many expenses. Not happening."

His daughter frowned at him, but he continued to ignore her. "We don't need a fancy fridge, merely a big box that keeps things cold. If I can find something on a good deal that would be worthwhile and has some extra features, maybe I could get it. But for now, forget it."

The conversation ended after that, and he resumed his search. Alexis gave up and returned her focus to her phone while Vickie chatted with Eric.

Eric: *Everything getting back to normal?*

Vickie: *Kinda. Alexis and I are at least talking once in a while*

Eric: *Good. Maybe having her dad back will help*

Vickie: *We'll see.*

Eric: *Oh geez*

Eric: *You haven't been on FB yet have you?*

Vickie: *Not yet. Only in Messenger. Why?*

Eric: *Remember what they did in gym class?*

Vickie was confused. How could she forget what they did to her in gym class? She opened her Facebook app and dreaded to see what was going on.

When her feed loaded, she sighed loudly. Dozens of students from Clear Lake High School had changed their profile pictures to clown noses. A handful of them—including Megan Fitz and Abby Fontaine—bombarded her account with pictures of clowns and Rudolph the Red-Nosed Reindeer.

Vickie: *Rrrrrgh*

Vickie: *It's like I can't get away from this*

Eric: *They are relentless*

Vickie: *Makes me want to stay home from school—it's not like I'm offended by it, but I'm getting really tired of it*

Eric: *I know*

Eric: *I am too*

Vickie: *I would give anything to go a week without having to deal with all this clown stuff*

Eric: *Why don't you tell somebody?*

Vickie: *Like who?*

Eric: *I don't know—Principal Goede? There has to be something someone can do*

Vickie: *idk, I think that would make everything worse*

She didn't want to tattle on the rest of the class, even though all she wanted was for them to stop. But telling on them would open a new round of ridicule, and she would cement her status with them for her entire high school future.

Instead, she rolled onto her back and stared at the ceiling with a scowl.

Craig looked up from his computer and immediately noticed that she seemed agitated by whatever was going on in her head. "Are you okay?"

"I'm fine." Vickie stood, picked her phone up, and walked to her room.

Craig looked at his daughter. "How's it going with you two?"

Alexis didn't look at him. "I don't know. We fought most of the weekend and didn't talk to each other much. But I don't know what's bugging her lately. It seems like she's on edge."

"And you've not talked to her about it?"

"Dad, I'm doing my best." She finally looked up. "If I'm part of the reason why she's upset all the time, me talking to her won't do any good. Why would she talk to me?"

He frowned at her, closed his laptop, and slid it into the magazine rack next to his chair. *Time to go back to being a father again.* He stretched his legs, walked to Vickie's room, and knocked on the door.

"Yeah?"

"Can I come in?"

"Sure."

She was lying on her bed, still typing to Eric. She

looked visibly irritated but remained quiet when he walked in.

"Tell Eric you'll talk to him later. I want to have a chat with you."

"Okay." She ended the conversation and pushed her phone away. "What's up?"

He sat on the edge of her bed. "So what's the deal lately? You've seemed really irritated by everything. Alexis says you two have been fighting too. What's on your mind?"

"It's nothing." She shook her head and shrugged.

"Obviously, it's not nothing. I can tell when something is bothering you girls. Both of you wear your hearts on your sleeves, which is great for me as a parent but terrible for you when you don't want to talk about it. Come on."

Vickie sat and slid over so that her back rested against the wall at the head of her bed. "One of the girls at school took a photo of me before I covered up a big zit on my nose last week."

"Okay…"

"And since then, they've shared it on Facebook, called me a clown, and joked about me being Rudolph. The whole gym class showed up with clown noses one day and now, they're all making clown jokes on Facebook."

Craig tilted his head forward. "That's it?"

"What do you mean, that's it? It's driving me crazy!"

He scratched his head. "I don't mean to be insensitive, but you're a vampire. You've had people surround you and try to cut off your head. Literally. A few kids make fun of you and that bothers you this much?"

"You don't understand. When people threaten me physically, I can retaliate. Those scumbags from the Circle?

They needed to die. Killing them wasn't an issue because they were trying to kill me. It's not like I can walk through the school and get back at them physically."

Craig nodded. "No, you definitely can't do that. But them making fun of you bothers you this much? Why?"

"I can't get away from it! I go to school five days a week, and somebody is always making some kind of joke about it now. They follow me around. I come home, and the second I go on Facebook, I see someone else has made some snarky comment about it. I'm so tired of being around it that I'm going crazy. I don't know how to stop them."

He folded his arms. "Okay, now I get it. Well, there's good news and bad news. The good news is that you can get them to stop. The bad news is that you'll have to look like a fool to do it."

"What do you mean?"

"Do you promise you won't repeat this story?"

Vickie shrugged. "Sure."

"I mean it. Not even to Alexis. She doesn't know this one." She nodded, so he continued. "When I was in middle school, I completed a spelling contest and won a free lunch from Burger King. As you can imagine, for a kid, this was a huge deal. All my friends packed peanut butter sandwiches, and I would get to eat a hot burger and fries in the cafeteria, along with a tall soda."

She laughed. "Big man on campus."

"You bet. And I lived it up in the days leading to it. All that morning, I talked about how excited I was for lunch. When it arrived, I smelled it, waved it around, talked about how good every bite was, and made fun of everyone else's pitiful lunches. Mmmm-mmm. It was fantastic."

"I'm sure you were really popular then."

"Oh, the kids hated me for it. I couldn't blame them, looking back. I was a total jerk to anyone who would listen."

"So you were the bully?"

"Nope, this story gets much worse. After lunch, either the food didn't sit right with me or I was sick with a stomach bug. Regardless, I found myself in a position where my stomach started to hurt. Pressure really built up in my system, and I needed relief."

"What does that mean?"

"I passed gas. A lot of it."

Vickie covered her mouth and tried to stifle her laughter. "Are you really telling me this story?"

Craig got a little red in the face. "I'm not proud of it at all. Seriously. If I didn't think it would help you, I would keep it to myself. Anyway, it was only a little at first, but then it continued for the entire afternoon. I couldn't stop. There was no hiding it, either. Sometimes, you try to be cool about this stuff but it's unavoidable. It was loud, and it was obvious. By the end of the day, the other kids were either laughing at me or complaining about it. I was helpless."

"Oh, boy." She placed her hand on her cheek. "I can only imagine how much you were made fun of."

He nodded sadly. "For two weeks after that, I was Burger King Boy. Every opportunity they had, the other kids brought it up in conversation and had a big laugh over it. They constantly joked about it, even when no one said anything about food or smells or whatever. It followed me wherever I went."

She began to see where he was going with it. "But how did you get them to stop? Or did you?"

"Oh, I did. I had to go nuclear."

"What does that mean?"

With a smirk, he continued. "I went to the store and bought a shirt that said Burger King on it with the logo and everything. It was a dorky shirt, but I had to make a point. I wore it proudly to school for a week, and by the end of the week, the jokes stopped."

Vickie's lip curled up. "How did that make them stop?"

"Because I took away their ammunition. Bullies like to get a reaction. That's the reason they do it. If it bothers you, they'll keep going. But if you can make yourself a part of the joke, you'll win."

"How do I do that?"

"I don't know." He stood from the bed and slapped his thighs. "You'll have to think of that yourself. I'm happy to help in any way I can. If you can think of a way to take the joke away from them and make it your own, they'll stop. I promise."

CHAPTER TWENTY-THREE

J im fidgeted nervously with his hotel room key as he sat in the lobby of the Radisson and stared at the entrance doors. Pete walked in and saw him waiting.

"Hey, where've you been?" He greeted the newcomer.

"I ran across the street to the mall to pick up a few things but mainly, I wanted to walk around a little. Who are you waiting for?" He spun around to look at the entrance.

He sighed. "Bob Quinlan."

Pete looked at him and raised his eyebrows. Bob Quinlan was the head of the Oversight Department at the CIA. Whenever an agency needed funding or approval for projects and investigations, they had to run it through him.

"Are you...I mean, what's he here for?"

"Probably looking for an update." He glanced at his hotel room key. "He didn't want to do it on the phone. That's never a good sign."

His colleague shrugged. "Try to stay positive. Maybe he

needs some evidence. Do you have everything you need? Do you want me to stick around?"

"No, I rented the conference room here." Jim pointed to the door behind them beyond the ice machines. "I have the meter in there, some paperwork, and all our findings so far."

Pete took a deep breath. "When was the last time you met with Bob?"

"When he fired me from the Zombie Army project." He nodded slowly with his lips pressed together. "He actually wanted to meet me to shut the whole department down, but I managed to sweet-talk him into keeping it open. That's how I came up with the whole balloon thing."

The plastic bag in the other man's hands crackled as he folded his arms and it bounced against his side. "Hey, that balloon thing is why we're here. That was a heck of an improv. You do your best thinking when your back is against the wall. Maybe you can knock this one out of the park. We've made solid progress. He'll see that."

"I hope so."

Pete slapped him on the shoulder. "Stay confident. If he senses you're hesitant, he'll shut you down. You'll do great. Call me if you need anything and I'll come down. I'm not going anywhere tonight."

"Thanks, Pete. Have a good night."

As the man walked to the elevators, Jim returned his gaze to the door. He realized he was slouching and wanted to appear strong, so he pushed himself upright, squared his shoulders, and puffed his chest out. *No, that's not confident enough.* He stood from his chair and stretched his back. To stop fiddling with his hands, he stuck his room key in his pocket.

As he did so, a stern-looking man with gray hair parted to the side and weathered features walked through the entrance. He wore a nondescript black suit and black tie with a crisp white shirt.

"Mr. Trembo." He walked directly to Jim and extended his hand.

Jim mustered a confident-looking smile and shook his hand. "Mr. Quinlan—Bob—it's great to see you again."

"I doubt that very much. Where would you like to meet?"

"Oh, I have a meeting room set aside over here. Follow me." He led him to the door of the meeting room, pulled out his hotel key, and swiped it to unlock the latch. When he pushed it open, he gestured for Bob to walk in first.

"Thank you." The man stepped in and immediately saw the meter on the table in the middle of the room. He glanced over his shoulder to make sure the door was shut behind them. "This is the electromagnetic meter that we commissioned for this project?"

Jim stepped forward eagerly and placed his hands on the burned-out device. "Yes, sir. As you can see, it's been through the mill." He pulled off the outer chassis to reveal the charred machinery beneath. "We brought this meter to the middle of the field where we first detected the activity. I hoped that we could measure the flare-ups as we investigated, but we weren't there more than ten minutes before all the gauges went wild. The machine began to smoke and eventually, it failed."

Bob nodded. "Definitely evidence of something being off, that's for sure." He sat at the table across from him.

Before he'd sat properly, Jim began to pass the paperwork in bundles. "Here, we have the original readings from the balloon project and our initial photographs. We're still investigating some of the pieces that we found at the scene, including this ancient sword. We believe that all of this together offers legitimate proof that we're on the right track here. Honestly, I haven't seen this much evidence stacked up so quickly in all my time with the department."

He waited for some kind of answer or reaction. Bob leafed quickly through the papers before he tossed them on the table. "I'm not here for proof today, Jim. We're getting the reports. We believe that you've found something substantial here."

A weight fell off his shoulders and he exhaled quietly. "That's great. We're all on the same page. But then...why are you here, Bob?"

The man folded his hands on the table in front of him. "Jim, we want to know what you plan to do with this information. What are your next steps?"

"Oh..." Jim looked at his papers, then at the meter. "Well, we've ordered another meter and we'll resume our excavation of the site itself. I want to know exactly what kind of creature we're dealing with here, and—"

Bob raised his hand to keep him from continuing. "I understand that, Jim. But let me rephrase the question. The Ghost Plane project had a clear line from investigation to military use. You thought we could either develop technology that would aid us in war, or we could take advantage of whatever supernatural phenomenon caused it to attack our enemies without putting soldiers' lives at risk."

"That's right." He nodded. "I still think that one could've worked out."

"Nevertheless," his superior continued, "the reanimation project was a little more out there, but you had built up some goodwill with the department and we trusted that you knew what you were doing. And again, there was potential. Reviving soldiers during wartime and putting them back on the battlefield offered limitless potential."

"I'll admit, the failure of that one really stung." Jim hung his head. "I thought that would be a major success if it paid off."

"I agree. It also stung the taxpayers who funded the project." Bob coughed.

"Do you want a drink of water? I can run out and grab you one." Jim saw it as a moment to collect his thoughts and buy him some time.

The other man seemed to read his thoughts. "No, thank you for the offer. We trusted you on both those projects because, despite the rather unbelievable opportunities they presented, we could easily see how they would benefit our military goals. But in this case, we're merely working off evidence of supernatural activity. What is it exactly that you believe is happening here in Milwaukee?"

Jim's eyes widened with determination. "The elevated electromagnetic activity tells us that a supernatural being is residing here somewhere. They've left evidence behind, and it is still rather potent, given that it blew this meter up."

"I agree."

"Our plan is to determine where this being is located, if there are others, and what kinds of supernatural powers or attributes they have."

"How does this turn into usefulness to our government, then?"

He began gesturing with his hands. "Think about it. When I spoke with Pete Stabone, one of my men, I used this example—say we have a werewolf-like creature at our disposal. We could potentially create an army of them. And for the sake of argument, we know that the werewolves can only be killed by a silver bullet. Opposing forces would not be able to feasibly stop a force of these creatures attacking them. If we have them on our side, we become unstoppable."

Bob narrowed his eyes. "Are you talking about forced breeding?"

Jim tilted his head, a little surprised by the question. "Well...I guess it could. But if they're going to breed anyway, maybe we can encourage it—like animals at the zoo. We can't force them, but we can certainly create a monitored environment where this can happen."

"So you want to put these beings or creatures in cages."

He ran his hands nervously through his hair. "Don't think of it like that. We only want to monitor them. It's a matter of control. You're thinking of it like enslavement. I think we can take advantage of whatever creature or being this is and use them to further our goals. That's all. Like the Aswang tribe in the Philippines."

The other man smirked at the reference. "The fake vampire."

"Exactly. If we can put a real vampire or werewolf or

whatever monster on the battlefield, who knows what we could accomplish?"

"And you're confident that this is actually a creature and not some other kind of supernatural activity?" He arched his eyebrows skeptically.

Jim pounded his fist on the table. "I know it. Finding that sword in the field meant something happened there. You don't bring a sword unless you're fighting something. At some point recently, there was a fight in that field between whoever wielded that sword and a supernatural being. Once we determine the origins of the weapon, I bet we can find out what we're dealing with."

After leaning back in his chair and staring at him for a moment, Bob stood. "You have time, Trembo. We're willing to give it to you. But that's if you can find a way to subdue whatever creature this is and put them to work for us. If you can't control it, we can't fund it. We won't throw millions of dollars at something that will end up killing all of us."

He stood quickly and extended his hand. "I understand. Good to see you, Bob."

His superior merely nodded at him and walked out of the room without even looking at his hand, much less attempting to shake it. Jim put his fists on his hips and turned to look at the burned-out meter.

I'll find this thing and get it under my control if it's the last thing I do.

CHAPTER TWENTY-FOUR

Vickie smiled as she zipped the extra duffel bag sitting next to her backpack. She hoisted it onto her shoulder, brought it out to the kitchen, and dropped it on the floor before she prepared a bowl of cereal.

As she wolfed her breakfast, Craig walked into the room. "G'morning."

"Morning. Hey, thanks for taking me to the store last night." She pointed to the bag.

He rubbed his face in an attempt to wake up. "It wasn't exactly how I wanted to spend my Sunday night, but I'm glad we were able to find the stuff that you needed." He indulged a loud yawn. "You're not wasting any time with this, are you?"

She swallowed a mouthful of her cereal. "No chance. I want to nip this in the bud, and that means starting as soon as possible."

He laughed. "I guess you're really taking my advice to heart. It's nice to see you excited to go to school for a change."

Vickie lifted the bowl to her lips and slurped the last of her cereal and milk. "If being ridiculous will make this work, I'm all over it. I want to end this."

"What's in the bag?" Alexis strolled into the kitchen and immediately noticed the extra luggage.

"Ammo." The vampire winked at Craig, who chuckled and shook his head as he walked away.

They arrived at school and she immediately walked to the locker room. She dropped the bag on the bench in front of her locker and took a deep breath. *Here goes nothing.*

After yet another deep breath, she hauled a large polka-dotted onesie out of the bag and set it aside with a bright red afro wig. At the bottom of the bag was a small white disc of face paint. She took this over to the mirror and began to apply the paint to her cheeks. When she noticed how bright the paint was, she smiled.

With her face now completely white, she painted the areas around her eyes a bright red, drew big ridiculous eyebrows on with a black pencil, and took a step back. *Not bad for an amateur.* She slipped into the onesie and zipped it, then grabbed the wig and moved to the mirror. Carefully, she tucked her hair into the wig. The sight in the mirror made her laugh.

Oh, I almost forgot! She scrabbled in the side pocket of the duffel bag and located a bright red rubber nose. Vickie slipped it on over her nose and gave it a squeeze. The nose emitted a piercing squeak, and she clapped with satisfaction.

Showtime.

After she'd tucked her change of clothes into the bag

and put it in her locker, she pulled the backpack on and walked confidently out of the locker room and into the hall. *Confidence. You're in on the joke. You look ridiculous and you know it. Don't let the laughing get to you.*

The hallways erupted in laughter combined with strange looks from her fellow students. The vampire deliberately took a long route along the halls to make sure she walked past Megan Fitz and her group.

When the girl saw her approach, she turned to Abby with her jaw hanging open. "What is she doing?"

Her friend shook her head. "What a moron. Hey, nice outfit, clown! You look stupid!"

With the biggest smile she'd ever had, Vickie turned to the group and squeezed her nose twice. The loud squeak sounded almost strident in the hallway. Several students laughed, and she skipped happily toward homeroom.

But by first period, the teachers weren't so amused. One of them took her aside and told her she needed to change.

"I know, but I'm trying to do something here. Can you please let me keep it on?"

The teacher—Mrs. Callahan—bristled at the suggestion. She was an old, conservative teacher who didn't like class clowns. "I hear what you are saying, but there has to be a better way to accomplish whatever it is you are doing. You are a distraction to the rest of the class. Please return to the locker room and change your clothes. I will excuse you from this period."

Vickie walked through the empty halls on her way to the locker room. *Hey, I got out of class for free. That's an added bonus.*

After removing all her clown getup, Vickie tucked the rubber nose in her pocket. Throughout the day between classes, she would walk into the hallway, affix the nose to her face again, and wink and smile at anyone who stared at her.

By gym class, she needed new material. She pulled Krista aside while they were getting changed. "I need you to do me a favor, but you have to do exactly as I say."

Her friend shrugged. "No problem. What do you want me to do?"

The two of them hung back in the locker room until almost everyone was out on the gym floor.

"Where are Vickie and Krista? I saw them in the locker room." One student looked around, confused.

"Probably hiding out of embarrassment," Abby laughed. "She looked ridiculous this morning. That strategy backfired!"

"Ho! Ho! Ho!"

The class turned to see Krista wearing a Santa hat and a big white beard, holding onto the reins attached to Vickie's shoulders. The vampire wore the big red nose again but this time, she'd attached giant antlers to her head.

Together, they galloped around the gym while Mr. Kolander looked on, completely befuddled. "Okay, okay... that's enough." He walked over to the two of them. "I don't know what's going on, but did you get it out of your system?"

"Yes, sir." Vickie smiled. "We made our point."

I will never understand teenagers. "All right. Go ditch this stuff and get back here so that we can get class going. We'll start without you."

As they made their way across the gym and back to the locker room, Abby looked on in disgust. "What are you doing, anyway?"

Vickie paused and stepped over to the towering teen. "You were right, Abby. My nose did look terrible. I looked like a clown. And I thought, if everyone thinks I'm a clown, I'll be a clown. If everyone thinks I look like Rudolph, I'll be Rudolph. Why not? I'm simply having a little fun. You should try it sometime."

The girl shook her head while the other two returned to the locker room.

The girls laughed when they were out of the gym. "What was all that about, anyway?" Krista asked. "Why are you pointing out that you looked like Rudolph in that picture?"

"Because then I'm in on the joke and that makes it less funny." She nodded confidently and dropped their costume items into her locker, although she tucked the nose in her pocket.

That day, they continued their study of volleyball. Whenever she saw Abby lining up to serve, Vickie would pull her nose out, attach it to her face, and squeeze it. The loud squeal that followed inevitably forced the girl to fumble her serves.

Once, she hit the net. With another attempt, she over-shot the court. Every single time, Vickie got under her skin. And when Mr. Kolander wasn't looking, she'd slip the nose on again and play volleyball with it on, laughing as she did so.

When class was over, the two girls walked to the locker

room together. Krista was beaming. "You really got to her. That was fun."

"It's not over yet, either. Wait until tomorrow."

Abby caught up with Vickie and blocked her path. "You still looked stupid. It doesn't change the fact that you are a clown."

"Just wait, Abby." She gave her a playful wink.

That night, she couldn't wait to tell Craig how things went. He was eager, too. "It sounds like you got the job done. Way to go."

"Not quite. I haven't used the last thing yet."

Craig winced when she mentioned it. "Are you sure you want to use it? If you already have the upper hand, it might be overkill. You don't need to take on unnecessary embarrassment."

"I feel empowered now, Dad. This is merely the victory lap." She walked away to her room, while he laughed quietly.

You're being a good dad here, boy. She's starting to learn.

In her room, Vickie logged onto Facebook and smiled when she saw all the students whose profile pictures were still full of clown noses. She rubbed her hands together and with a few clicks, updated her own profile picture to one of her in a clown nose and full clown makeup.

That is a hideous picture. It's perfect.

Throughout the evening, she remained logged in and watched as one by one, students changed their profile pictures to something cool or flattering. The clown noses disappeared.

Even in the comments on her picture, one student

wrote, *Eh. It's not as fun if she's in on it too. Party's over, guys. Time to find something new.*

Another wrote: *That didn't last long. Oh well.*

Vickie almost bounced with energy. She had taken the driver's seat of the conversation.

The next day, she walked into the school building, pulled her jacket off, and hung it in her locker. She spun around to reveal a shirt with the offending photograph of her zit blown up and highlighted across the front.

When Alexis saw this, she covered her mouth in horror. "Are you nuts? Do you really want to draw attention to that picture all over again?"

"Trust me. That's exactly what I want to do."

She moved from class to class, proudly displaying the photo. By the end of the day, she could overhear other kids getting tired of it.

"Ugh. Enough with the zit picture already."

"That was fun for like ten minutes."

"Move on. The joke's old."

With each complaint, her smile grew wider. She strolled past Megan and Abby at their lockers and tilted her head. "I guess the joke is over. Find something new to laugh at."

"You still look stupid." Abby sneered at her.

"Maybe. But now, no one is laughing except me. I'm not sure what a mic drop is, but I think this is one of those." She sauntered away, leaving the two girls fuming.

CHAPTER TWENTY-FIVE

The vampire felt like she was dancing on air when she packed her bag that Friday morning. Her sister stood in her doorway and watched her gleefully prepare to spend the night away from home.

"I have to say, it doesn't seem like that big a victory." Alexis twisted her face in confusion. "You made them stop talking about your nose. Big deal."

Vickie laughed and shook her head while she tucked a pair of shorts into her bag. "When half the student body is focused on something of yours that's embarrassing, come back and talk to me. I know it wasn't much, but it drove me insane. Now it's done and I am free to enjoy myself tonight."

Alexis stepped into the room and tucked her hands in her pockets. "Yeah, about that... I really want to warn you one more time. Tricia and that whole family are bad news. If you go there, you'll get sucked into something you don't want to be in. Really."

She tried her best to keep from losing her patience with

her. "I know you're trying to look out for me, but I don't need to be looked after. I can make my own decisions. If this is a bad idea, I would know it by now. I can sense that Tricia is a well-meaning girl who simply wants me to have a good time and relax. That's all we'll do."

"But you don't even know what she means by have a good time and relax. There are many bad ways that can go." She stepped in closer. "I'm not worried you'll *die* or anything but I don't want you to end up with the wrong crowd."

Vickie stopped packing and looked at her. "What's the right crowd, Alexis? Who should I hang out with? If I could get a list of friends who are approved by you, that would really help me."

Her sister sighed, genuinely frustrated. "I can't control what you do or tell you who you can or can't hang out with. I'm only trying to help." She walked out of the room.

The vampire stared at her back and shook her head. *I have to make my own decisions. At least I didn't fight with her this time.*

Tricia told her to meet her at the south entrance to the school building once the last bell rang. As she walked that direction, Vickie smirked when she thought about the fights she'd had with Will at the south entrance. *It's the perfect cover back there. She must be getting picked up there.*

When she pushed open the door leading outside, she saw Tricia puffing frantically on a cigarette. "Hey! You made it. Sorry, I get so anxious during school. I gotta have one before the ride home. Do you want one?"

"Oh…no thanks." She hadn't tried to smoke, but she knew enough from her education that it was a bad idea.

Plus, she wasn't too sure how vampires reacted to addictive substances and she wasn't interested in finding out.

"Okay, no problem. Let me finish this and we can go upstairs." The end of the cigarette glowed as she inhaled.

"We're not getting picked up down here?"

"Nope, my bro picks me up at the main entrance out front. I come down here to have a quick puff. No one ever comes down here after school. You'd be surprised what you can get away with."

Vickie nodded politely. *Yeah, well, you'd be surprised what I've already gotten away with, actually.* At first, the smoking bothered her, but she was able to rationalize it. *She's not pushing me to smoke. I said no and she respected it. That's all that matters.*

Tricia dropped the butt of the cigarette on the ground and stepped on it while she blew the last wisp of smoke into the air. "Ahhh, that's better. It takes the edge off. School is stressful enough, right?" She laughed. "We'll head back to my place and hang for the night. Maybe watch a movie or something."

"That sounds great."

"Come on." The girl opened the door and they walked inside and up the stairwell to the main level. By the time they reached the front entrance, an old white 1998 Buick Skylark was waiting for them. Inside, an older boy with a long goatee and dark sunglasses leaned back and stared ahead with an angry expression on his face and a cigarette hanging out of his mouth.

"What's up, Jay?" Tricia opened the passenger door and pointed to the back seat for Vickie. The vampire climbed in and slammed the door.

"Hey."

"Troy, this is Vickie. Vickie, this is my brother Troy."

She smiled. "Hi, Troy, nice to meet you."

"Yep." He blew smoke out the window and threw the car into Drive. As it lumbered out of the parking space, Tricia grabbed a cigarette out of the pack of Marlboros in the console and lit it with a lighter.

I have a weird feeling about this. Vickie shifted in her seat. *I'm not sure why. She's being really nice to me, though. Maybe it'll turn out fine.*

They reached a small duplex on the corner of a neighborhood block. Troy parked the car and exited without saying a word. As the vampire climbed out of the back seat, she couldn't help but notice all the garbage blowing around the street. *Boy, I thought our neighborhood got trashy. There are all kinds of garbage here.*

Across the street, two little girls played on the sidewalk, bouncing a basketball to each other. The house next to them had boards nailed on the windows and a sheet of paper taped to the front door.

"Come on, let's go in." Tricia waved politely as she flicked her cigarette into the middle of the street. They walked through an old gate that creaked and sagged.

Vickie pointed to a black sign with bright orange letters that said *BEWARE OF DOG* as the other girl closed and latched the gate. "Oh, you have a dog?"

"Nope. We put that there so people think we do. It helps to keep them off our property. Otherwise, they cut through our lawn, swipe stuff…you know."

The back door of the house opened to a stairwell connecting the main level with the upstairs and the basement. When they opened the door, Troy was already halfway down the stairs to the basement, an open beer in his hand.

"Geez, Jay, pace yourself. We're here too, you know."

He preceded his reply with a belch. "Shut up."

Tricia shook her head. "He's so selfish. He lives in the basement. You won't see him for the rest of the night. Eventually, he'll pass out. Come on, I'll show you around."

She led Vickie to a small living room that was packed with old furniture and a sixty-five-inch 4K TV. An older, wrinkled woman with dyed blonde hair sprawled on the couch, sleeping with her mouth hanging wide. Several empty cans of beer stood on the coffee table in front of her beside an ashtray with what appeared to be twenty or more crushed cigarette butts.

"This is the living room. That's my mom." Tricia walked in, located the remote, and turned the TV volume down so that the sounds of *Jeopardy!* wouldn't drown them out.

"Does she work late?"

The girl gave her a weird look. "No."

"Is she not feeling well? Or does she work hard during the day?"

Tricia looked at her mom, then at Vickie. "Oh. No, she doesn't have a job. She lives off child support from my dad, wherever he is. She's usually conked out by now. It's actually really cool, because then we're free to do whatever we want for the rest of the night."

She showed Vickie two small bedrooms and a bathroom that had evidence of several water leaks staining the ceiling.

"My room is upstairs. Let's go." Tricia led her up the

stairs to an entire upper-floor apartment. The layout mirrored the one on the main level, although it looked much different. The kitchen area was overloaded with boxes and other junk. Papers were stacked on top of the oven. "I don't use the kitchen much, but I do use the fridge. If you need anything, it's in there. I have food in the cupboard next to it, too."

Vickie nodded and walked over to the fridge to investigate. When she opened it, she was surprised to see only soda and cheap beer, along with two bottles of wine. Without saying a word, she closed the door and followed the other girl into the rest of the house.

The back bedroom was storage, where junk and clothes had been piled. The bathroom upstairs looked no better, although the countertop overflowed with bottles of various hair and skin products.

Instead of two bedrooms, this level had only one bedroom and a main living area. In the latter, Tricia had a large queen-sized bed, messy and unmade, and a small loveseat beside it. An old TV rested on top of her dresser, and her desk was also piled high with books and papers.

The vampire walked through carefully and looked around. *It's sloppy, but it's fine. It looks like she watches movies, so that's cool. I don't always make my bed either.* As she approached the nightstand, she saw another pack of cigarettes and an ashtray, a few empty beer cans, and several used cereal bowls.

"You guys sure like to drink and smoke, hey?"

Tricia laughed. "Oh yeah. Well, there's not much else to do around here. It's cool if you don't. I don't mind. I'm not like that. I thought we'd hang out, watch some movies, talk…all that jazz." She plopped herself on the loveseat. Vickie put her bags next to the bed and sat on the loveseat too.

The musty smell of old laundry piled high next to the furniture almost drove her to twist her face in disgust, but she tried desperately to be polite.

"It sounds like you really nailed everybody on that nose thing." Her companion straightened, excited, with a big smile on her face. "I'm impressed. Where did you come up with the idea to do that?"

"Alexis' dad, actually." She nodded and related how he'd convinced her to give it a try. "I decided I had nothing to lose. Everyone was making fun of me already."

Tricia stood, jogged into the other room, and returned with a beer in her hand. She cracked it and slurped the bubbles. "You know, I thought everyone overreacted about that nonsense anyway. Like, who cares if you have a zit? I have zits. Everyone has zits. Abby and those girls are dumb. I'm glad you shut them up."

Gradually, Vickie grew more comfortable. *This is why you hang out with her. So she does a few things that you don't. Who cares? She cares about you and how you handle life. That's what matters. No one is perfect.*

CHAPTER TWENTY-SIX

As the evening wore on, the effects of the drinking started to take their toll on Tricia, and Vickie took notice. She began to slur her words slightly, but it was her demeanor that caught her off-guard.

After the third or fourth trip to the fridge, Tricia brought back two beers instead of one and handed the second to Vickie. "Oh, sorry, I said I didn't want any."

"Relax, it's Friday night. Just drink." She wasn't smiling.

Sensing a little danger, she opened the top of the can and pretended to take a sip. *You don't know how you'll react to this, so pretend you're drinking. This isn't the environment to try.* "Do you have anything to eat? We haven't had dinner."

She waved her hand lazily. "I don't really eat dinner. I simply eat whatever. You can go get some food if you want." She pointed to the kitchen area.

The vampire stood and walked into the kitchen carrying her beer. Because she was out of view, she could dump the alcohol down the drain and pretend to drink it.

Rifling through the cupboards, she only found a few bags of chips and a box of popcorn. Seeing a microwave on the counter, she decided the popcorn would be a safe bet. *There's no telling how stale any of those chips are.*

Within a few minutes, she returned with a can of soda and a bag of popcorn. The other girl said nothing but she grabbed a handful of the snack every now and then as they talked.

Tricia put an old romantic comedy on the TV for background noise, but she continued to talk over it. "This is weird for a Friday night for me."

"Oh yeah?" Vickie took a sip of the refreshing—and much safer—soda. "What do you usually do on Friday nights?"

"Well, my boyfriend Alex usually comes over for the weekend and we hang out. I told him you were coming over and that he should stay home tonight. He was so mad."

"I'm sorry, I didn't mean to interrupt anything."

"Nah, don't worry about it. He's a big baby when he doesn't get his way. Yeah, he's only mad because he's gotta stay at home with his dad, and he hates his dad." She burst out laughing, but Vickie wasn't entirely sure what was so funny about that statement.

"You hang out here and watch movies?" She pointed to the TV.

"Yeah, sometimes. Maybe turn some music on. Smoke a little. Drink until we pass out."

That's...it? That's what she does with her time? Her mom and brother are there drinking themselves into a coma, and she's up here doing the same thing with her boyfriend? "You don't go out and do anything?"

Tricia slurped the last bit of beer out of the can in her hand, squeezed it, and tossed it onto the floor. "I can't do any of the fun stuff out there."

I hope she only means the drinking and smoking. I don't even know where I'm going to sleep tonight. Is this really all there is? Do I have to squeeze up on the loveseat? Or share the bed with her? Do I have to sleep on the floor next to all the beer cans and who knows what else?

A sinking feeling overcame her and she grew anxious. Her blood began to race through her veins, as the fight or flight response in her body heightened. *I'm in a little danger here. I need to get out as soon as I can.*

She sat quietly and bided her time, watching the movie on the TV. Out of the corner of her eye, she could see Tricia's head nodding. *If she falls asleep, I can get out of here.*

After a moment, she stood to walk toward her bag on the floor next to the bed. A groggy Tricia straightened and looked at her, confused. "Where are you going?"

"Oh...I'm going to get another beer."

"Sweet. Grab me one too." The girl sagged on the seat and rested her head on the back. Vickie walked into the kitchen to pretend to get a beer, then peeked around the corner to see Tricia out cold.

"Sorry, Tricia," she whispered as she retrieved her bags and slipped out the door. She walked down the stairs and out the back door, knowing that no one in the house was conscious enough to notice.

The vampire stood on the curb and looked at the house. *She meant well. She really did. But she has much bigger issues to deal with than I do. Maybe I can help her someday, but it won't be tonight.*

She noticed several groups of guys walking around and shouting loudly at each other on the street. With a deep breath, she bolted into the night, wanting nothing more than to go home.

While she wasn't quite sure which direction to go in, she had noticed how they got there from the school, so she ran to the school and stopped a block shy of it. No one was around that late at night, so she could finish her sprint home.

Vickie arrived home on the back step at 11:30 p.m. She unlocked the side door and tried to push it open, but the chain attached to the door frame stopped her.

Footsteps charged through the house. She peered through the open door to see a confused Alexis.

"What are you doing home?"

"Let me in, please."

"Okay, back up." Her sister pushed the door closed and unhooked the chain. When she opened it again, she looked worried. "Are you all right? Is something wrong? Are you sick? Did something happen?"

"I'm fine. I only…it was a bad idea. I need to go to bed."

"Okay." Alexis didn't say another word. She could tell the other girl wasn't in the mood to talk.

Vickie went directly to her room and shut the door behind her. She sat on the bed, dejected. *I made a choice, and it was the wrong one. I don't know what to do. Am I stuck simply hanging out with Alexis' friends? Why is everything so complicated here?*

On the other side of the hallway, Craig was dealing with his own struggles.

He lay in bed, staring at the opposite side where Carol used to sleep. His mind raced with thoughts of his interactions with Chelsea at the convention. Every time he thought of her, his mind turned quickly to Carol, and he felt guilty all over again.

I'm sorry, honey. I feel like such a cheater. You haven't been gone that long and I was already looking at another woman. It's not fair to you or your memory.

As he piled the guilt onto himself, he drifted off to sleep and had a vivid dream.

He stood in a lush, green park in the middle of the day. The sun was shining overhead. The air was so perfect and calm that he didn't know where his skin ended and the fresh air began. A small pond stood in front of him, and to his left was a park bench.

An iron sign was affixed to the back of the bench. He leaned over and squinted to read it.

SIT.

Craig looked around and saw no one in any direction. He sat on the bench. The sunlight reflecting off the pond water was so bright, it almost blinded him. His eyes watered while he squinted, and his vision became blurry.

After blinking a few times, he noticed a figure standing before him. He couldn't quite make her out yet, but he recognized long, dark, curly hair, full lips, a brilliant smile, and a flowing white dress.

She came into focus, and he lost his breath. It was his wife.

Her hands were folded in front of her, and she looked down with relief to see him. "Craig."

"Carol." The word barely escaped his mouth.

"Now, I can't stay long. I wanted to say hi." She stepped to the side and the brightness of the reflection on the water subsided.

He couldn't take his eyes off her. She looked glorious. Her skin was bright and healthy. She wasn't withered away like she had been during the last months of her life. She was vibrant, radiant, and stunning.

Carol sat beside him on the bench. His lips parted slightly, in awe of her presence once more.

"I've been watching, Craig." She smiled at him. "You're doing a wonderful job with Alexis. It looks like she's really growing up strong."

"I…uh…I'm doing my best. I don't know how well she's turning out. She really misses you. I really miss you." His bottom lip trembled.

She patted him on the thigh. "Hang on, don't get all blubbery on me yet. We have to have a little talk. First, Alexis. She's doing really well, and you're doing great. This parenting thing is hard, especially for somebody doing it on their own. Don't sweat it. Listen to your instincts."

"You were my instincts."

Carol laughed and the sound sent a wave of joy through his heart. He longed to hear that laugh again. "No, I told you what to do all the time. You still have those instincts. You simply have to listen to them. And you are. That's good."

He wiped a tear away and tried to focus on savoring this moment. "Sorry, I just…how is this happening?"

She glanced at the sky above them. "I worked something out with the Big Guy. It seemed like you needed a little guidance. Now, back to business. This Vickie girl...it is so sweet of you to raise her and take care of her."

Craig shook with nerves. He didn't know what to do with his hands, so he rested them awkwardly on his lap. "She didn't have anyone, Carol. I was only trying to do the right thing."

"That's why I fell in love with you in the first place. You always try to do the right thing. And you're doing great with her too. I know her being a vampire really mucks things up, but keep going. It'll pay off."

His limbs turned to Jell-o as she took his hand. He squeezed hers like he always did.

"Finally, let's talk about what happened in Chicago."

"Honey, it meant nothing. I was merely talking to a woman. I don't even know how it happened."

She lifted his hand and placed it on her heart. "Craig, you are the most loyal, faithful, and loving man I ever met in my life. In all the years we were married, you stood by my side, even when I was sick."

"I took a vow, Carol. I would always be by your side."

She nodded. "Right. But when I died, that vow was no longer binding. We're not married anymore. We can't be."

He released a small sob. "I sure wish we were."

Carol tilted her head sympathetically. "I know. I do too. But this is where life has gone. And the one thing you always cared about was my happiness. Now, I want you to be happy. Do you think I want you to sit around moping for the rest of your life? Do you think Alexis wants you to be unhappy forever? Get out there and meet people. Date.

Have fun. You're not cursed to be alone indefinitely because I'm not there anymore."

Craig placed his hand on top of hers, then moved to grasp hers with both hands. "I don't know how to be happy without you."

She wrinkled her nose playfully at him like she always used to. "That's because you haven't tried yet."

"I don't want to replace you."

"Well, shoot, Craig. I'm not saying replace me. There's no replacing me." They both laughed. "Craig, moving on with your life doesn't mean you forget the past. But don't let the past dictate your future. I'm releasing you of your guilt. Go. Date. Have fun. Please. Do it for me."

He leaned back on the bench and stared into her eyes. "Can't I stay here?" He laughed, already knowing the answer.

"Someday, you will." She squeezed his hand again. "But your job isn't done yet. You have a girl down there—two girls, actually. They need you to be there for them and guide them. When your job is done, you'll come here and we can pick up where we left off."

Carol slid over and rested her head on his shoulder, bringing a wave of happy memories to him. "I would give up everything I own to be able to do this with you again and again. I sure wish you could come back with me."

"I know, but rules are rules, honey. I have to stay here, and you have to go back." She raised her head and brushed his cheek with her fingertips. "But know that I'm still here, I'm still watching, and I'm still by your side. You're never alone in this. And give yourself a break. You're a good man and you always have been. Don't let guilt ruin your life. You have no more obligations to me, okay?"

"I love you, Carol." He sighed out of pure emotional exhaustion.

She smiled at him. "I love you too, Craig." She tilted her chin up to kiss him. He leaned in eagerly to return it, and she turned to kiss him on the cheek.

Then he woke, tears still streaming down his face.

CHAPTER TWENTY-SEVEN

As Craig struggled with his dreams, Vickie tossed and turned as well.

The events of the evening had bothered her, and she didn't quite know where to turn anymore. Depressed, she sank into bed but couldn't fall asleep.

Staring up at the shadows on the ceiling distracted her and reminded her again of the other night when she accessed the long-buried memory of the day she found out her siblings were dead.

Can I get to earlier in that day? Can I find out what they did that caused me to be so mad at them? Maybe if I knew that much, I could at least forgive them or something. It bugs me that I was so mad at them when they died.

Squeezing her eyes shut, she was able to transport herself back into Salzburg four hundred years before. She was in the same day as before, but earlier. And this time, she was in the middle of a forest.

Vickie looked around to see if she could find her younger counterpart. A blur *whooshed* past her and almost knocked her off her feet. *Relax, these are only shadows. But I think I know what shadow that was.*

Without hesitation, she tapped into her super-speed and raced in the direction of the blur. Soon, she caught up to a giggling Young Victoria, who ran alongside her brother and sister. They laughed and pushed each other around the way they always had.

She instantly began to cry with a smile on her face while she watched the camaraderie among the three of them. *That bond...I really miss it. We were so close.*

Occasionally, one of them would run into a tree because they weren't paying attention. Some trunks tipped slowly. Others fell in swift crashes. Regardless, the fun didn't stop between them.

Vickie continued to run with them, enjoying the sight of the family fun. *This is exactly the kind of thing I can't do with Alexis. We loved horsing around and being vampires together.*

She missed the family bond of the vampire race.

Still, her excitement was tempered by the knowledge that this was the day her brother and sister would die. What she enjoyed were the shadows of their final moments together.

Her brother stopped the group and turned his head as if he tried to hear something. His mouth hung open slightly, and he took both sisters by their hands. "Come with me."

"But I still want to play," Young Victoria begged.

"Sister, come with me. Now." He was stern and forceful.

The village was near the forest, and he took them directly there, moving as quickly as he could without actually tapping into his speed. All the while, his head swiveled in all directions, trying to determine whether or not they were being followed, or so it seemed.

When they reached the village, he sat both girls down at the water pump. He stooped to meet them eye-to-eye and raised his index finger. "You both stay here. Do not move. Okay? I will come back and get you later. Stay right here."

Neither girl replied as he walked away from the village and back out into the fields until he was out of sight.

Victoria's sister refused to comply and stood immediately. "I'm going with him."

"But he told us to stay here."

Vickie smirked. *What a little rule-follower I was.*

"No, he's hiding something. I want to know what. I'll go get him. I'll be right back." She walked away without looking back and was barely out of the village when she burst into the distance and out of view.

The vampire watched as Young Victoria rested her chin glumly on her knees and watched the villagers walk back and forth.

They left me. That's why I was mad at them. They left me in the village. She looked at the position of the sun. *It's still morning. Vater didn't come for me until the afternoon. I sat in that place all day long, waiting for them to return, but they never did.*

She felt guilty for being mad at them. *I was only a little kid. But I should've known better. I should've realized that something was wrong. My brother wouldn't abandon me like that. My sister wouldn't either. But why did he leave us there? Did he know he was going to die? If he did, he wouldn't have said he would be right back.*

Her stomach tied in knots, she gazed off into the

distance where her brother and sister had run off. *Don't linger. If you go too far, you'll see things you do not want to see.*

Ignoring the inner warning, she set off in that direction until she caught up with her brother, who marched into the forest. With another *whoosh*, her little sister arrived at his side.

He immediately panicked. "What are you doing here? Go! Go back to the village. Please."

She folded her arms obstinately. "No! I want to know what you're doing. You're hiding something from us. I'll tell Mutter and Vater that you're being naughty."

He crouched, placed his hands on her shoulders, and shook his head nervously. "No, I'm not. I'm trying to protect you. Please, go back before—"

Out of the woods, a group of black-cloaked men approached the two young vampires. Vickie's stomach dropped when she saw the glint of the sword blade the Circle had tried to use to kill her.

She looked at her brother and sister, who now clutched each other in fear. *Oh, how I wish I could step in and save you both. I wish this didn't have to happen.*

He looked at his little sister and nodded. "Run."

The two of them burst away, and the Circle raced after them. Vickie now refused to follow the shadows.

I don't know where they catch up to them. I don't know how they catch them. I don't know what kind of fight they put up. I don't know their last words.

I don't want to know any of it. All I know is how it ends, and that's enough for me.

She snapped back to the present day, sat up in her bed, and took a few deep breaths to calm herself.

They didn't abandon me. They were trying to protect me. He was trying to protect me. My brother left me there because he wanted to save his sisters. I was mad at him for keeping me alive.

I should have been dead along with them. Oh, my poor parents.

Her heart continued to race, knowing how close she was to witnessing the demise of her siblings. But as she thought about them, she noticed the parallels between them and Alexis.

In the morning, she got up before everyone and cooked breakfast. Her sister emerged from her bedroom first and sniffed the air.

"Good grief, I smell bacon, eggs…and what else?"

Vickie smiled and pointed to the oven. "Cinnamon toast."

"What's the occasion?" She sat at the table.

The vampire set down the spatula on the countertop and turned to her. "Forgiveness, I hope."

"For what?"

"Two things. First, I should have told you about Will. I put you in danger, which I had no right to do. If I'm going to be your sister, I have to look out for you." She sat beside her. "Deep down, I didn't think Will would try to hurt you. I thought he only wanted to hurt me. But that's still no excuse. I'm sorry."

"It's okay." Alexis nodded. "I know you didn't mean to put me in danger. I was upset, I think, because my first boyfriend turned out to be such a bust. I should've listened to the warning signs."

Vickie took another deep breath. "And speaking of

warning signs, the second apology. I should have listened to you about Tricia."

The other girl leaned in. "Yeah, what happened last night? You came home and went to bed without saying a word. I thought you were staying there."

"Me too. But then she started drinking heavily."

"Ugh." Alexis winced.

"Yeah. And it's not like it was a party or some kind of social thing. She simply drinks all the time. And smokes, too. The place was filthy, everyone was drunk, and I had such a bad feeling about the situation. I should have listened to your warning signs."

"I'm glad you got out of there before anything bad happened."

"Me too. And here's a bonus third apology. I'm sorry I got mad at you at all. You're only trying to help me. Sometimes, I can't see what somebody is doing to protect me, and it feels like they're simply trying to control me or punish me. I need to be able to step back and see the bigger picture in these situations."

Alexis pulled up her ankles and tucked them under her knees, rocking back and forth in the chair. "You can't always see that. Nobody can. I think it's just more important that we do a better job of communicating without letting our emotions get out of hand."

Vickie nodded and stood to return to the hot pan on the stove.

"And you're right about one thing."

"What's that?" She stirred the eggs.

"You do need to have friends who aren't mine. You have

to have the chance to go out and bond with people independently. I can't protect you from that."

The sound of a doorknob clicking interrupted the conversation and Craig emerged from the bedroom wrapped in a blue bathrobe. "Good morning, girls. Wait… Vickie? Aren't you supposed to be at a friend's house?"

"It didn't work out." She flipped the sizzling bacon.

He looked at his daughter, then back at her. "Are you okay?"

"I am now. Everything's fine. I simply want to eat a good breakfast with my family." She served the eggs and bacon from the pans onto plates, then pulled the cinnamon toast out of the oven.

With a warm smile, she sat at the table with them. "Dig in. Thanks for being my family."

Alexis shrugged. "I don't know what's gotten into you, but if it means more eggs and bacon for us, I can get on board."

Craig looked at his two girls, proud at how they had apparently worked out their problems. He glanced at the sky and nodded at Carol before he turned his attention to his plate.

CHAPTER TWENTY-EIGHT

"Welcome back to the world of distance running, everybody!"

"Yeah! Woo!" One of the senior boys clapped in excitement as everyone in the room laughed.

"Thanks, Chris." Lueck laughed at him as well. "So, this is track season, and I know we're officially getting started a little later than usual this year. Most of the season has been bumped to the summer thanks to the inclement weather we've had. But hey, we're here, and I know most of us have been running all winter anyway."

He scanned the room. "There are a few new faces, so while you're out on your runs today, make sure you introduce yourselves. We're all a team here. It's a beautiful day to put in a handful of miles, so I want you all to break into your teams and go run five. We have a meet in two weeks, and I want to make sure everyone is in tip-top shape, ready to compete. There are many races to squeeze in."

The group dispersed, and Krista stopped in the hallway. "Shoot! I forgot my watch in my locker."

Vickie smiled. "I'll wait for you."

"Sweet. Thanks. I'll be right back." She jogged into the locker room while the rest of the girls' team headed out the door.

For a minute, she was alone until Coach Lueck walked past. "Is something wrong? Why aren't you out with the girls?"

"Oh, nothing's wrong, Coach. Krista forgot her watch so she's hurried back to get it. I thought I'd hang back and wait for her."

"Okay, no problem. Are you glad to be back in running season?" He rubbed his hands together excitedly with a huge smile on his face.

She shrugged. "I guess so. Not as much as you, apparently."

"Ah, think about it, Vickie—fresh air, good exercise, and great friendships. You can't beat it. Have a good run." He jogged away to catch up with the boys' team.

He's right. There are good friendships on this team, aren't there? I was so worried about fitting in that I never really noticed. Krista even dressed up like Santa Claus for me. That's a good friend right there.

The locker door clunked as it swung open, and Krista jogged out with a watch strapped to her wrist. "Sorry about that. Thanks for waiting. Ready?"

"Let's do this." Vickie followed the other girl out the door.

When they reached the parkway behind the school, they looked in either direction but couldn't see anyone. "Shoot, I don't know which way they went. I guess we'll have to go off on our own." Krista smiled.

"That's fine with me." She nodded and the two of them began to run.

After a few minutes of silence, the vampire decided to take advantage of the opportunity. "What do your parents do for a living?"

"That's a random question. My mom is a nurse. My dad is a cop." Krista huffed and puffed as they picked up the pace. "Yeah, Mom worked half-time while raising me and my siblings, but then went back full-time after we were in school."

"It sounds like they are really smart." *Medical people know so much. Police officers have to know all the laws. It's good to see someone whose parents have good heads on their shoulders.*

"Yeah, they're smart. But they also work hard. That's what they always taught me and my brothers."

Okay, even better. They work hard and are responsible. Good influences. "Are you close with your brothers?"

"Oh yeah. They can be jerks sometimes, but you never get along with your siblings all the time, you know?"

Vickie laughed. "Boy, do I know that."

"But we love each other. There's nothing I wouldn't do for them. My older brother, Micah, is in college studying to be a teacher. My younger brother, Jesse, wants to be in the military someday but he has some growing up to do yet. Maybe he'll change his mind. I don't want my little bro to be in a war or anything."

She loves her brothers and gets along with them. Her older brother is working on his future. Very good.

"What's with all the questions?" Krista furrowed her brow. "These are coming out very suddenly."

Think fast, Vickie. Don't tell her you're vetting her for

friendship. That's lame. "I'm...starting to ask more questions now, that's all. Since I came here from Austria, everyone always asks me loads of questions about my home life that I have to answer. I'm returning the favor for whoever wants to tell me about their lives. I like to learn about people." *That's a weird, rambling answer.*

Despite the awkwardness of the explanation, Krista didn't question it. She was cool with it, which made her relax.

The two of them enjoyed their run together. Although they missed the first workout with the team, they gotten to know each other quite well—more than they had during the entire cross country season.

"I thought you were kind of quiet when you joined cross country this year." Krista smiled. "Like, I knew you were nice and all, but I wasn't sure if you were outwardly friendly or if you were kind of weird or what the deal was. But since we've had gym together and I've got to know you more, you seem normal."

I hide the weird stuff well, I guess. "I always thought you were cool, but I have to say, you earned tons of cool points from me lately."

"How so? Let's attack that hill over there and make this a workout."

Whatever you say. I can pretend I'm working harder. "You did that Santa Claus thing with me in gym class. There aren't many girls who would wear a big white beard in front of their fellow students like that. It was a really goofy thing to do."

They reached the base of the hill and paused to catch

their breath. Krista stopped her watch. "I don't mind being goofy. I actually kinda like it. Being goofy is fun."

"You don't care what people think of you?"

She shrugged. "Sometimes I do. It depends on the situation. But life is more fun when you don't care what people think about you. That's why I liked doing that Santa thing with you. It was silly and would have been embarrassing if somebody made you do it. But you were doing it willingly, which was like a big 'I don't care' to everybody else. Plus, it shut them up about the stupid zit, which was totally a giant waste of time for everyone."

She has a great perspective on life and her reputation. I like that. "It's fine, I wasn't terribly crippled by it. But like you said, they wouldn't shut up about it. It was way better to take charge of it, laugh about it, and move on. My dad taught me that."

Krista stretched her hamstring and prepared to sprint. "It sounds like you have a good dad then." She pressed the start button and the two girls raced up the hill, slowing as they reached the top—one voluntarily and the other involuntarily.

"I could tell all that stuff was still bugging you, though, and I was tired of seeing that." Krista gasped. "That made me happy to do anything I could to help you get through it and move on. You're fun when you're in a good mood, and those girls made it impossible for you to be in a good mood."

She cares about her friends and wants to see them happy. Very thoughtful.

The duo sprinted down the hill and instead of stopping at the bottom, they continued down the parkway.

By the time they returned to the high school parking lot five miles later, Vickie was all smiles. "That was fun. I almost didn't want it to end. It was nice to do a one-on-one run for a change."

Krista put her arm around her and pulled her in for a sweaty hug. "We have a few years of running left in us. There will be many more opportunities."

After the girls changed in the locker room, Vickie thought about taking a chance. "What are you up to Friday night? Do you want to hang out?" *Maybe this friend will turn out a little better than the last one.*

"I'd have to check with my parents, but I'm sure it's okay. It sounds like fun."

She cares what her parents think. And more importantly, her parents care where she is. "Oh, shoot." She snapped her fingers. "I'm working on Friday night. I can't, actually. Unless you want to hang out at a fish restaurant."

"Ummm...pass." They both laughed.

"What about Saturday night? I know I'm not working then. My sister is working, so I'll be bumming around the house."

Krista nodded. "That sounds good. I can get a ride. What time?"

"We'll go to the Brewers' game during the day, so it would have to be after that. Maybe six or seven."

"Ooo, a Brewers' game. Have you been to one yet since you moved here?"

"Not yet." Vickie shook her head. "I'm looking forward to it. It should be fun."

"They are fun. I love going down to Miller Park. You'll

have a blast and you can tell me all about it on Saturday night. I'd love to hear an outsider's perspective."

The vampire practically danced to the car, she was so happy. *I'd been looking for a friend of my own, and I had one right under my nose this whole time. And she's awesome. It's shaping up to be a fun weekend.*

She climbed into the SUV, where Craig waited with a smile. "Hey, Vickie. How was your first track practice? As good as cross country?"

"It was different." She buckled her seat belt and slid her bag to the floor. "But it was great fun. I think it'll be a really cool season."

"I'm happy to see you enjoying school again. I was tired of seeing you have a hard time with everyone."

She looked out the window at the sun setting in the distance. "I know. I simply had to be around the right people, that's all."

CHAPTER TWENTY-NINE

The massive yellow letters spelling out *MILLER PARK* hung over Vickie's head as she stared at them after she scrambled out of the car.

"Thanks, Mom!" Eric hunched over and stuck his head in the car window. "I'll text you when the game is almost over."

"Have fun, kids. Behave." She drove off, leaving Eric, Vickie, and Alexis standing on the sidewalk in front of a big statue of a rather average-looking man.

"Now, I'm already confused." Vickie pointed to the statue. "I expect statues around a baseball stadium to be of players—guys playing baseball in uniforms. This guy is standing there in a polo shirt and pants. Why does he have a statue?"

Eric walked up to it and patted it on the shoe. "This, darling, is Bob Uecker. He is the pride and joy of Milwaukee baseball."

"Was he a great player?"

Alexis laughed. "No, actually he was terrible. But he's

our commentator on the radio. He does the play-by-play for people listening to the game. He's really funny."

"Yeah, he was also an actor." Eric stepped back and looked at the statue of the smiling jokester. "Hilarious guy. He was in *Mr. Belvedere* and the *Major League* movies."

"I don't know what any of that means." She shrugged.

Her sister put her hand on her shoulder. "I can't promise you *Mr. Belvedere*, but we can watch *Major League*. It's a classic movie."

"You know that was filmed here in Milwaukee, right?" Eric walked away from the statue and they headed to the line to get into the stadium. "They had an old ballpark here called County Stadium, and they filmed many of the games there. It was where Little League Park is now." He pointed to a small ballpark in the middle of the sprawling Miller Park parking lot.

"That's interesting." Vickie nodded. "So they film movies all over the place, then? Not only in Hollywood?"

"You know, Vickie, I'm surprised my dad hasn't told you about *Major League* already. He loves to tell new people about it. Like, two blocks away from our house is this temple, but in the eighties and early nineties, it was a restaurant called the P'Zazz. They filmed quite a few of the restaurant scenes from *Major League* there, and it's down the road from our house."

That news actually impressed both Vickie and Eric. "That's really cool. We'll have to watch it so I can see."

After they entered the park, Eric excused himself to use the bathroom. The girls waited in the concourse, as streams of people filed in to watch the game.

"Alexis, I want to triple check with you—are you sure you're okay with being here with us?"

"Why wouldn't I be?" She giggled.

"You know. Because we're dating and I don't want you to feel awkward."

She rolled her eyes. "Vickie, as long as you two don't make out in front of me, I'll be fine. Don't worry about it. Let's have some fun. It's a baseball game, it's a beautiful day…it doesn't get better than this."

"Let's eat." Eric clapped enthusiastically as he walked out of the bathroom. The trio visited a booth called AJ Bombers and ordered Wisconsin burgers—a slab of ground beef topped with white cheddar cheese, bacon, and fried onions.

Paired with tall sodas, the burgers were excellent and filling.

Of course, not everyone was full. Vickie was ready to eat more. "Maybe some ice cream? Or fried cheese curds?"

He laughed. "Let's get to our seats first."

"Oh, sure." She walked away from them and toward the open air of the park. *That's where they play, so our seats must be right around there.*

Eric ran after her and grabbed her arm. "Sweetie, our seats aren't there."

"They're not?"

"No. Those are seats behind home plate. They're hundreds of dollars apiece. Unless the fish place starts paying you five hundred dollars an hour or something, we won't sit there anytime soon. Come on."

They returned to Alexis, who led them to the escalator.

"We're in the Upper Deck, Vickie. We have a few escalators to ride."

After several minutes of walking and climbing, they finally reached their seats near the roof of the stadium. Vickie marveled at the height. "This place is huge. The players look so tiny from here."

"Yeah, my dad always calls these seats the nosebleeds." Alexis giggled.

"My family calls them the Uecker seats. Bob Uecker was put in upper deck seats in an old beer commercial from the eighties. You can find it on YouTube, it's actually quite funny." Eric walked over to the row on their tickets, and the three of them sat with Vickie in the middle.

"Beer here-uh! Get'cher beer here-uh!"

"Who's that guy?" Vickie pointed to the shouting man in a yellow shirt carrying a cooler strapped around his shoulders.

"That's the beer guy," Alexis answered. "He sells beer in the aisles so you can buy another drink without getting up."

"That's a good idea. Do they do that with anything else?" She looked quizzically at the man, while her companions exchanged amused looks.

"Yeah, they'll sell snacks and sometimes sodas. You'll see throughout the game." Eric put his arm around her. "I forget how much we take for granted when we've been coming to these games all our lives."

After everyone rose for the National Anthem and cheered on the first pitch, it was time for the game to start. The Brewers pitcher struck the first three batters out, and the crowd went wild for such a great start to the game.

As the first Brewer player came up to bat, Vickie's eye caught sight of a man in a big-headed costume stepping out onto a deck above the outfield. "What's going on there? Who's the guy with the big head?"

"That's Bernie Brewer." Eric smiled. "He's our mascot. That's where he hangs out while the Brewers are up. He keeps the crowd in the game and leads them in cheers and stuff. And then he celebrates whenever one of our guys hits a home run."

"That's funny. I hope they hit one so I can see it."

The game moved along rather quickly, as neither the Brewers nor the visiting Pittsburgh Pirates could muster any hits.

Between innings, a buzz ran through the crowd. "What's happening?" Vickie didn't hide her confusion.

The announcer's voice boomed: "Alllllllll right, fans, it's time for the Klement's Sausage Race!"

"Sausage Race?" Vickie curled her lip at Eric. "Those two words don't make sense together."

"Just watch. Come on, Bratwurst," Eric shouted and clapped loudly.

To Vickie's surprise, five people in towering sausage costumes walked out onto the field along the third base-line. She looked at the scoreboard and determined the competitors—Bratwurst, Hot Dog, Italian, Polish, and Chorizo.

A starter's pistol fired, and the people in the costumes sprinted down the line, around home base, and toward the first base.

"They look like they'll tip over. Do they ever tip over?"

Alexis shook her head. "Not usually. I think it's

happened, but it's rare." The Bratwurst won the race as Eric cheered, and Alexis remained standing. "I have to use the bathroom. I'll be right back."

After she left, Eric took the opportunity to pull Vickie in close and squeeze her hand. "It's fun having Alexis with us, but it's nice to have a quick moment alone with you."

She pointed to the big video screen. "We're not that much alone, actually."

He glanced up and laughed as the two of them were shown on the screen in a big pink heart frame with the words, *KISS CAM* plastered above them. He leaned in and gave her a big kiss, which made her laugh and blush while the crowd cheered them on.

Vickie couldn't stop giggling. "I wondered if we'd get the chance to kiss today, but that's not really what I had in mind."

"I know, but it's been a while since we've been able to hang out. With you working and Alexis' dad being gone... it's tough."

She punched him playfully in the shoulder. "Yeah, and Mr. I Don't Want To Run Track."

"Hey, I prefer cross country, okay?" He pulled her in tighter. "How is track so far?"

"It's great, actually." Vickie nodded. "I'm beginning to be good friends with Krista."

"Oh, that's good. Krista's cool. I always liked her."

"Yeah, she's coming over to hang out tonight after we get back from the game. Alexis has to work, so she'll chill with me. I don't know what we'll do yet, but it has to be better than my night with Tricia."

Eric shuddered. "No kidding." He loosened his arm

around her when he saw Alexis approach in an effort to not make her feel weird.

After a few more scoreless innings, the crowd rose to their feet. "Now what's going on?" Vickie looked around as music began to play through the loudspeakers.

"The Seventh Inning Stretch. Time to sing!" Eric rose to his feet and took her by the hand. They joined with the crowd to sing "Take Me Out to the Ballgame," which was immediately followed by accordion music.

Various couples in the stadium started dancing the polka, singing "Roll Out The Barrel" in unison.

"It's a Brewer game tradition," Eric shouted as he led her in a short polka trot before he hauled out his phone. "Speaking of tradition…"

As he typed out a text, the crowd sang "Zing! Boom! Tararrel!"

When the song ended, everyone sat once more.

"What was with the text, Eric?" Alexis leaned over.

"I always text *TARARREL* to my buddy Aaron whenever I'm at the game. And vice versa."

"That's weird."

He laughed. "I don't even know why we do it anymore. But we've done it for years. Tararrel!"

The Pirates players all struck out in the eighth inning, but the second Brewer batter finally cracked a home run over the wall. The crowd bounded to their feet and cheered. Vickie did too, excited to see the reaction of a Brewer home run.

Bernie Brewer climbed to the top of a large yellow slide and slid down as fireworks exploded over the stadium. He grabbed a huge Brewers flag and waved it excitedly while the crowd roared.

At the end of the game, the Brewers won, one-zero.

Eric and Alexis remained seated when the crowd started to rush to the exits.

"Why aren't we getting up?" Vickie wondered.

"There's no point." Her sister shook her head. "We always wait for the crowds to move through a little. Otherwise, you stand there waiting for people to walk."

The three leaned back in their seats, basking in the glow of a Brewers win, and watched the sky turn bright orange and purple. Eric stroked Vickie's hand with his thumb, and she smiled at him.

It was the perfect little afternoon, even if Alexis had to be the third wheel.

CHAPTER THIRTY

That evening, Krista and Vickie had a wonderful time hanging out, watching movies, and eating popcorn. It was the kind of evening the vampire had hoped for when she visited Tricia, but that never happened.

They stayed up late, talked about their lives, and Krista learned all about Austria.

By the time one a.m. rolled around, Krista snored on the floor of Vickie's room, but Vickie didn't sleep soundly at all. Instead, she tossed and turned as images flashed through her mind.

She saw herself locked in a cage, screaming to get out. Various faceless men and women in white coats walked past, looked at her, talked about her, and disappeared. Food would slide into the cage, and she would practically dive on it.

Once in a while, a man would walk up with latex gloves on, grasp her arm, and stab her with a needle. Sometimes, he would take blood. At other times, he would inject her with something.

Vickie ran from side to side in the cage, her teeth bared like an animal. She tried to bite the bars but to no avail. She ran as fast as she could at them, but they wouldn't give and she would fall back into the enclosure.

Then, in another flash, she stood on a stage in front of flashing cameras and people with microphones, a leash around her neck and her hands and feet chained together.

Her cheeks were stained with tears and for some reason that remained unclear, her body was filled with a heavy weight of depression—like she had given up on life entirely.

In another flash, bombs exploded mere feet from her, and she was shoved by soldiers to the front of the line of battle.

"Do I get a gun?" she screamed at them. "I can't defend myself."

"Go! Go! Go!" they shouted at her.

Unable to determine what was going on, she charged ahead in the direction they ordered. Bullets rocketed past her. She grunted in pain whenever one of them struck her.

Occasionally, the blast of a bullet bowled her over. Her face hit the sand, blinding her and filling her mouth. While she tried to muster enough spit in her dry mouth to eliminate the sand, the burly hands of the soldiers yanked her to her feet and pushed her forward again.

Exhaustion set in and she began to limp, trying to heal her constant bullet wounds but unable to maintain the effort.

Enemy soldiers that she couldn't make out attacked and stabbed her repeatedly. She cried in pain but no one tried to save her. Every time a soldier came near her, they simply hauled her to her feet and pushed her forward.

"Bite him! Bite him!" they screamed hysterically at her.

Through tears and slurred words, she tried to explain to them that she didn't bite. They wouldn't listen and forced her forward and on top of the enemy soldiers to try to force her to sink her teeth into them.

She wailed in fear, pain, and despair...and she woke in a cold sweat.

Once she realized where she was, she leaned over the bed to make sure that Krista was still asleep. She didn't want her to know anything about her vampire side. To her relief, her friend still snored loudly.

Carefully, Vickie stepped over her and walked out of the bedroom into the kitchen. She got a drink of water to relieve her imaginary dry mouth. Sweat rolled down the side of her head.

"Can't you sleep?"

She turned to see Alexis walking toward her, her arms folded in front of her.

"No. You?"

Her sister shook her head. "Not with that girl snoring away in there. It sounds like she's starting a chainsaw."

"Sorry."

"It's fine." She waved her hand. "I'm simply happy you have a good friend. Not that you need my approval or anything." She noticed Vickie didn't return the smile. "Are you all right? You look like you've seen a ghost."

The vampire placed her hand on her stomach and closed her eyes, trying to calm her body.

Alexis gritted her teeth. "I know that look. Something's up. What do you sense?"

Vickie opened her eyes. They were wide and her pupils were huge. "I don't know. But it's really, really bad."

"Okay, let's sit. Bring the water."

They sat at the table and she took another sip. "I saw some terrifying images in my head. I was trapped and treated like an animal or some kind of science project. They kept stabbing me with needles and parading me around in front of people with cameras."

Her sister leaned in and frowned. "Are you sure this wasn't simply a nightmare?"

"No." She shook her head emphatically. "I know what a nightmare is. This wasn't that. It was like a prediction. It was a vision of what might happen in the future. I was like a lab rat or something. But then…I was out on a battlefield. It was the middle of a war of some kind. I couldn't tell who the good guys were or who the bad guys were. I kept getting shot and blown up and then pushed forward again."

"That's awful." Alexis took a sip of water as well. "Are you afraid that this is what will happen to you?"

Vickie glanced out the window. "I don't know. I've had visions in the past. It's like…these are visions of what could happen if I make the wrong decisions. Or something like that."

"And you couldn't see who it was?"

"Nope. Everybody's face was hidden. I didn't recognize a soul. There were people everywhere, and they looked constantly at me but I couldn't see any of them. That was the scariest part. Something's coming, Alexis. I can feel it in my gut again. Bad things will happen."

Alexis took a deep breath. "Do you think it's the Circle? Will they come back to try again?"

She placed her hand on her stomach. "It's worse. Bigger than the Circle. More powerful than the Circle. And much, much more dangerous than the Circle."

Get sneak peeks, exclusive giveaways, behind the scenes content, and more.
PLUS you'll be notified of special **one day only fan pricing** on new releases.

Sign up today to get free stories.

CLICK HERE

or visit: https://marthacarr.com/read-free-stories/

For Hire: Teachers for special school in Virginia countryside.

Must be able to handle teenagers with special abilities.

Cannot be afraid to discipline werewolves, wizards, elves and other assorted hormonal teens.

Apply at the School of Necessary Magic.

AVAILABLE AT AMAZON RETAILERS

Find the compass, save the world or save herself?

Dating is harder for Maggie Parker than running down a felon. Now add in magic.

Did she just see a compass fly?

Can she learn how to use the magic of bubbles to chart a new course in time? It's a lot harder than it sounds.

Join her on her quest to rescue passengers on an ancient ship – a big blue marble called Earth – and save herself.

AVAILABLE ON AMAZON AND IN KINDLE UNLIMITED!

I was born under a wandering star, but I got a late start at the wandering part. Let me explain. For most of my life I have wondered where else I could be. Not because I hated where I was, although there were a couple places that I ran from as fast as possible, but most of the time it was because I wanted to know who else is out there? What are they doing? What fun and amazing thing can I find out by meeting them?

It's probably why I was a journalist for a long time and endured being on the road driving for hours, sleeping on narrow beds a lot just to get a good story. All worth it and then some. The stories I could tell you...

But for a while, for the sake of the Offspring, Louie, I stayed put in one spot. I planted myself so he could have a childhood with roots. The entire time I was itching to get the hell out of there. It didn't really help that I didn't exactly mesh with a small town in Virginia. Granted, my father's family has been from that area since about the

1600's or so and that may have also been part of the problem.

I once walked out of church in a large crowd and a very old woman at the front yelled out, "You're Cary and Bobbie's child!" My brain spun in that weird way it can do when something happens that just shouldn't be possible. You see, my grandfather, Cary Carr died in 1933 and my grandmother, Bobbie died in 1960 when I was six months old. So, a very elderly stranger saw my face in the back of a crowd and still knew who I belonged to. By the way, my mother had heard about it before I got to the other end of town.

Some may think that's fabulous! Such deep roots! But I was the proverbial square peg living around a lot of round ones. I'm interested in board games, and magic, and trompe l'oeil art and a really good book and ways to make things better. Somehow, I just didn't quite fit. Yeah, I needed to go somewhere and be anonymous for a bit. Figure out where I did fit or see if that was even possible. Was it even a goal?

Lots and lots of moves later, when someone asks – where are you from – I pick Chicago. It's one of my favorites and for a while I really put down roots… till I ripped them up and moved on a couple more times.

Then this wonderfully magical thing happened. Recently, I was away from this dream house that I moved into just last September, hanging out in Scotland with a lot of other authors. Normally, I like being away from the usual duties and come home feeling refreshed.

This time, despite the beautiful Scottish city of Edinburgh and the great time I was having, I missed my nest. I wanted to be doing things with my neighbors, hanging with my dogs, going through my usual routine.

Those feelings felt foreign and strange and it took me a while to realize, I missed home! Instead of wondering what new thing could I find out there? I was wondering, what deeper layer can I learn about where I am? What more is there to know right where I live? I found my spot!

I still don't know if you can ever go home again. But apparently, if you're open to it, you can finally find a home, at last. More adventures to follow.

THANK YOU for not only reading this story but these *Author Notes* **as well.**

(I think I've been good with always opening with "thank you." If not, I need to edit the other *Author Notes*!)

RANDOM (*sometimes***) THOUGHTS?**

Moose in the Air.

Ok, that needs a little context.

A few weeks ago, my wife (Judith) was watching *Comedians in Cars getting Coffee* w/ Jerry Seinfeld, and his guest, Kevin Hart.

Kevin mentioned a skit Jerry did WAY back in the 1980's related to Moose in the Air...Flying and Judith BUSTS out laughing, and I couldn't figure out why.

It wasn't that funny.

Fast forward a couple of weeks (and many, many times that I heard her say 'huh, I guess I can fly' and laughing a LOT right after), and I'm sort of complaining to Stephen

Campbell on an Operations call about this STUPID joke that makes Judith crack up so much.

So, while I'm kvetching about this, Judith FINDS a clip of the joke on her phone, and lifts it up to the video camera on the computer (we were ZOOMing a call (like Skype)) and we play it for Steve.

The only problem? The original skit video she found was actually a lot funnier than the piece I saw, and Steve thought it was funny.

(Editor's Note: It was *funny. Jerry does a good bewildered moose)*

https://www.youtube.com/watch?v=ygtzecPLCkU

AROUND THE WORLD IN 80 DAYS

One of the interesting (at least to me) aspects of my life is the ability to work from anywhere and at any time. In the future, I hope to re-read my own *Author Notes* and remember my life as a diary entry.

Paris, France

Lying in bed, watching the light at the top of the Eiffel tower go round and round at 12:22 AM in the morning.

A little way in the distance is the Arc de Triomphe, not as easily seen at this time of night. We are in a hotel in the La Défense area, and no, I have no idea what that stands for. It's probably something insanely cool and I have no clue.

Perhaps I should look it up... *One second.*

Ok, it's a big bust here. The area is merely a business district three (3) kilometers west of city center, and no indication (from my really quick Google-fu effort) as to why it's named La Défense.

(Editor's Note: The name of the district comes from the statue of La Défense de Paris *by Louis-Ernest Barrias which commemorates the Parisian resistance during the Franco-Prussian War. And BTW, from your other notes earlier this week, you can see the Eiffel tower from about 70km, weather and architecture permitting.)*

However, from the tenth floor of the Melia Hotel looking to the East, it is a beautiful view.

Should you be interested.

FAN PRICING

$0.99 Saturdays (new LMBPN stuff) and $0.99 Wednesday (both LMBPN books and friends of LMBPN books.) Get great stuff from us and others at tantalizing prices.

Go ahead. I bet you can't read just one.

Sign up here: http://lmbpn.com/email/.

HOW TO MARKET FOR BOOKS YOU LOVE

Review them so others have your thoughts, and tell friends and the dogs of your enemies (because who wants to talk to enemies?)... *Enough said ;-)*

Ad Aeternitatem,

Michael Anderle

OTHER BOOKS BY JUDITH BERENS

OTHER BOOKS BY MARTHA CARR

JOIN THE ORICERAN UNIVERSE FAN GROUP ON FACEBOOK!

CONNECT WITH THE AUTHORS

Martha Carr Social

Website: http://www.marthacarr.com

Facebook: https://www.facebook.com/
groups/MarthaCarrFans/

Michael Anderle Social

Michael Anderle Social
Website:
http://www.lmbpn.com

Email List:
http://lmbpn.com/email/

Facebook Here: https://www.
facebook.com/TheKurtherianGambitBooks/